SISTER

Giving out warmth and loving care to all her patients was not always easy, Sister Madeleine Carver found, especially when she received so little support in her private life. So Dr Christian Galantière's offer of a job in a private hospital on the Côte d'Azur seemed like an instant antidote . . .

*Books you will enjoy
in our Doctor Nurse series*

DR DELISLE'S INHERITANCE by Sarah Franklin
DOCTOR'S ROMANCE by Sonia Deane
BACHELOR DOCTOR by Leonie Craig
ORCHIDS FOR NURSE NOELE by Jenny Ashe
SURGEON IN DISGRACE by Lynne Collins
THE SURGEON AT ST PETER'S by Rhona Trezise
THE LEGEND OF DR MARKLAND by Anna Ramsay
SURGEON IN WAITING by Clare Lavenham
SURGEON'S AFFAIR by Elizabeth Harrison
THE CLASSIC SYMPTOMS by Grace Read
HIGHLAND HOSPITAL by Judith Worthy
DREAM DOCTOR by Margaret Barker
HEART OF A NURSE by Elisabeth Scott
NURSE ON APPROVAL by Jennifer Eden
THE DOCTOR'S VILLA by Jenny Ashe
SURGEON IN THE SNOW by Lydia Balmain
DOCTOR KNOWS BEST by Ann Jennings
SUZANNE AND THE DOCTOR by Rhona Trezise

SISTER MADELEINE

BY
LILIAN DARCY

MILLS & BOON LIMITED
15–16 BROOK'S MEWS
LONDON W1A 1DR

First published in Great Britain 1985
by Mills & Boon Limited

© Lilian Darcy 1985

Australian copyright 1985
Philippine copyright 1985

ISBN 0 263 75214 3

Set in 10 on 12 pt Linotron Times
03–1085–51,300

Photoset by Rowland Phototypesetting Limited
Bury St Edmunds, Suffolk
Made and printed in Great Britain by
Richard Clay (The Chaucer Press) Limited
Bungay, Suffolk

CHAPTER ONE

THE rain came suddenly, shocking Madeleine Carver out of her sombre reverie and drenching her thoroughly before she could begin to think of seeking shelter. She sighed and quickened her pace, thinking that after all a wet uniform didn't really matter. The walk from the hospital to the Nurses' Residence was not a long one and she would be able to change into dry clothes as soon as she arrived there.

The rain disturbed her more for other reasons. It was early May, but spring had seemed far wetter and more unpleasant than usual this year—or was it only that her low spirits had put a gloomy cast on the weather as on everything else? It had rained during the night, too, and she had woken, wondering whether she could bear many more nights of lying in the narrow bed listening to the gushing of the water against the metal of the drainpipe outside her window.

But this Tuesday morning had dawned fine, so she had not bothered to take an umbrella. The day on Women's Surgical B had been an absorbing one, and when she left the hospital building at a little after three, still thinking about the last patient she had tended, she had not even thought to glance up at the sky. It was worrying that this tendency towards abstraction seemed to be growing . . .

A large car pulled up at her side and its driver leaned across to open the door and speak to her. Madeleine recognised Dr Brownrigg. He was an old friend of her father's and, as well as seeing him and his wife occasionally for a meal or a weekend, she often encountered him in the corridors of the hospital, where they would exchange a smile and a few words.

'Madeleine! You're soaked!' he exclaimed now. 'Get in and I'll run you to wherever you're going.'

'Don't worry, Dr Brownrigg,' she replied, not moving to take the seat he offered. 'I'm just on my way to the Nurses' Home after an A shift. It's not worth making your car damp and muddy for such a short journey.'

She smiled as she spoke, but a sudden gust of wind slicing sharply through the drenched cotton of her uniform made her shiver uncontrollably, and Thomas Brownrigg frowned as he noted the white skin of her face and the contrast it made with the deep shadows that lay beneath her eyes.

'Nonsense!' he said. 'You're completely drenched, and you're shivering.'

He pushed the door open wider and Madeleine took her place reluctantly at his side, deciding that it would be ruder to continue to argue.

'How about coming home for tea with us?' the gruff-voiced doctor said now. 'Barbara hasn't seen you for weeks. She'll have a fire going, and something delicious in the oven, I've no doubt, and Jennifer left plenty of clothes when she went on her trip. You can borrow whatever you like to wear, while Barbara puts your uniform in the dryer.'

As he spoke he had turned up the controls of the car heater and pulled smoothly out of the hospital driveway, leaving Madeleine with little choice but to accept the offer.

And it did sound so inviting! Lately she seemed to have been spending practically every night at the Nurses' Residence in front of the television or in her room with a book, without a great deal of companionship. Most of the friends with whom she had trained did not live there now. They had gone to other hospitals near Sevenoaks, or to other cities, or had moved into shared flats. Some lived with their families as Madeleine herself had done until six months ago, and one or two were married. Besides, no matter how pleasant and how much fun it was, a nurses' residence was never like home.

How much more enjoyable it would be to spend an evening with the Brownriggs, listening to Barbara's bright chat about the latest exploits of her four adventurous children and toasting herself by a real fire instead of feeling only the prosaic warmth of electric heaters. Madeleine began to look forward to the evening so much that she forgot to talk, but Dr Brownrigg did not mind. He was content to take stock of her appearance and manner as they drove, and he found that he was worried by what he saw.

It was six months now since Peter and Jean Carver had died so tragically in a weekend road accident. For several days Madeleine had been distraught with grief, but suddenly and just as dramatically she had pulled herself together, repressing and hiding her feelings, firmly refusing the offer of a home with Dr and Mrs Brownrigg, and moving into the Nurses' Residence while she wound up her father's and stepmother's affairs under the guidance of the family solicitor.

Madeleine's elder brother Richard had only been able to afford a week's visit home from the Middle East where he worked as an engineer for an oil company, and so by far the heaviest burden of the whole terrible business had fallen on the young nurse's shoulders, as she juggled her time between work at the hospital, sorting through her parents' possessions, and dealing with the sympathy of distant relatives which, though sincerely meant, was often more of a trial than a comfort to her. Now at last everything was settled, and Madeleine's life had assumed the outward appearance of normality and of a regular routine, but Dr Brownrigg was still worried about the girl.

The colouring that she had inherited from her Irish mother—sooty black hair and long dark lashes fringing deep blue eyes—only accentuated her pallor, and she had very definitely lost weight. She seemed lifeless somehow too, in marked contrast to her former warm, vibrant cheerfulness.

'How are you enjoying the hospital?' Dr Brownrigg broke the silence with the question and took keen note of her reply—not just the words, but the gestures and expressions she made as she spoke.

'Fine!' The bright smile accompanying a vigorous nod did not reach her eyes, and she did not manage to suppress a sigh after the short reply. Dr Brownrigg made no comment, however.

'And what about other things? Social life?'

'Oh . . . quiet. But I've never been one for a heavy night-life,' she said lightly.

'Nevertheless . . . How old are you? Twenty-one?' Dr Brownrigg responded to Madeleine's evident desire to keep the conversation away from anything too serious by using a teasing tone himself. 'You have to get out, get away from the hospital sometimes.'

'Oh, of course. I went to a film last week, with Andrew Forbes . . . a radiologist. I think you know him. And coffee the week before that with Dr Bari.'

To Dr Brownrigg it did not sound like enough. At twenty-one, with no ties, and—it appeared—no steady boy-friend, even a serious and sensible young woman ought to be going out and seeing more of life than that. Making a dispassionate assessment, Thomas Brownrigg could see that Madeleine was a very attractive girl indeed, even now when not at her best.

The creamy skin and black hair were an unusual combination, and though the bone structure of her features was a little too angular for some tastes, it was finely drawn. The doctor was quite certain that there were many men at the hospital who would be more than happy to have that intelligent face and compact though curved figure at their side on any social occasion.

He guessed, however, that it would be quite a battle for any man to make an impression on Sister Carver in the withdrawn and unhappy state she seemed to have fallen into. She was gazing—or rather, staring blindly—out of the window now, evidently satisfied that she had answered his questions sufficiently well to deflect any anxiety he might have been feeling. In fact, she was quite wrong.

The cosy evening at Thomas and Barbara's fulfilled all Madeleine's expectations, and she returned to the hospital, after spending the night in Jennifer's vacant room, feeling more cheerful than she had done for weeks.

Unfortunately this state did not last beyond a few days of hectic and sometimes discouraging work on Women's Surgical B. It was not that she was unhappy in her work. In fact, at times over the last six months it was only an utter absorption in work for eight hours every day that had kept her sane and in control, she sometimes thought. But going on with the same round of activity day after day, giving out warmth and care to all her patients and receiving so little support in her personal life . . . it was very difficult.

When Dr Brownrigg sent a message through the hospital courier system asking her to come and see him in his office after work on the Monday following her evening at his house, her heart lifted as she thought of what it might mean. She *was* depressed, and very likely that fact had not escaped the notice of the perceptive doctor. Was he going to renew his offer of a home with himself and Barbara in their cheerful house that was almost in the country? This time, Madeleine thought, she would probably accept. Pride and a determined independence had led her to refuse the offer the first time it was made, but loneliness and unresolved grief were stronger feelings within her now, after six months.

As she hurried along to his office at three, four hours after receiving his summons, she was already imagining how the garden would look in summer from Jennifer's big south-facing window . . .

'Ah! You're looking brighter this week,' were Dr Brownrigg's first words as he greeted her. 'The weather has improved. Is that it?'

'I expect so,' she nodded with a smile, wondering whether to sit down in the one easy chair that sat cosily in a corner. She had been on her feet since seven that morning. He gestured towards it a second later and she sank gratefully into its depths.

'I wanted to see you because I think you may be able to help out a friend of mine,' Thomas Brownrigg said, without preamble.

Madeleine's heart sank at the words. They certainly did not sound like the prelude to the offer she had been imagining. Tears of disappointment pricked hotly behind her eyes, and she had to force down a growing lump in her throat, chiding herself inwardly at the same moment for having let her fantasy about living with the

Brownriggs grow so uncontrollably in such a short time.

'His name is Christian Galantière—Dr Galantière,' Dr Brownrigg was saying now. 'He's a very capable surgeon and is in charge of the surgical section of a highly-regarded private hospital in the South of France—on the Côte d'Azur. One of their nurses has just left at very short notice and they're looking for someone to replace her as soon as possible, before the summer season gets into full swing. Dr Galantière is in England at the moment for a conference. We had dinner together on Saturday and he happened to mention his problem. He said that they would prefer an English nurse who speaks good French, as they have a lot of English and American tourists down there. I thought immediately of you. I thought you might feel like a change, and as I said, it would be helping Dr Galantière out . . .' He paused.

Madeleine was stunned and speechless. It was the last thing she had expected to hear, and for the moment she could not think rationally about the idea at all. Leaving St Catherine's where she had trained, leaving Sevenoaks and England altogether, going to a warm climate. The South of France—a strange country. Would it be lonely—or excitingly new? 'As soon as possible.' Speaking French.

Dr Brownrigg cut in on her chaotic thoughts.

'Don't feel that you have to give me an answer now. And if you're interested, Dr Galantière will of course want to interview you. I told him you might be able to go up to London on your next day off.'

'You've told him about me?'

'Yes. I made no commitment on your behalf, though, naturally. But I told him how highly you were regarded here. He asked about your French, and I said I thought it would be adequate, and that I was sure you would be keen to work at it if you did decide to go. You did your A level in it, didn't you?'

'Yes. And I've had two holidays in Brittany with . . . Father and Jean, as well as a school trip to Paris.' Madeleine finished the phrase quickly after her hesitation.

'Good. Dr Galantière will have to make the decision, of course, but he seemed to think that you sounded capable enough.' Dr Brownrigg paused. He was being less than honest, but he suspected somehow that if Madeleine knew how the conversation had really gone, how in fact he had asked Dr Galantière to take her on as a personal favour to himself, she would not want to take the job . . .

'When do I have to give you an answer?' Madeleine was asking now in a quiet voice.

'When is your next day off?' Dr Brownrigg returned.

'Thursday.'

'Then I'm afraid, my dear, you'll have to think it over tonight and make up your mind by tomorrow.'

He was very sorry himself that this was the case, as he was afraid that with so little time to consider the offer, Madeleine would decide to play it safe and refuse, yet Christian had been adamant. He wanted to interview any applicant personally, his schedule at the conference next week was very heavy, so interviews would have to take place this week, and if he could not see Madeleine within the next couple of days, he would go to an agency, ask to see several women, and make his choice from amongst them. Dr Galantière, Dr Brownrigg reflected, was a man who liked to set his own terms and make his own decisions.

'Yes, I see,' Madeleine replied after a pause to Dr Brownrigg's last statement. 'So I should come to see you tomorrow afternoon to let you know what I've decided?'

'Yes. Then I'll contact Dr Galantière on Wednesday and arrange a time for you to see him.'

'Very well, then.' Madeleine stood up to leave, her thoughts still in too much of a turmoil for her to think of asking about how Barbara and the children were. Dr Brownrigg realised that all she wanted to do was to go away and think, so he did not offer her coffee, contenting himself with saying:

'I'll hear from you at about this time tomorrow, then?'

'Yes. Goodbye.'

Madeleine left the rather dark office and walked in a daze to her room in the Nurses' Residence, where she changed into casual slacks and a pullover and made herself a cup of tea, only being able to think rationally about the new possibility that had opened up when she was sitting comfortably and sipping the hot brew.

The corridor was quiet. Many people were at work, others were out for their days off, and most of those who had been on an A shift like herself had gone out somewhere to do shopping or meet friends for afternoon tea. Madeleine thought that practically every other occupant of the rooms on this floor would jump at the opportunity she had just been presented with, yet she hesitated.

The Côte d'Azur! It would be easy to believe that going to a place so renowned for glamour and beauty would be an instant antidote to the dreariness that had invaded her life and her spirit. It would be easy to dream of excitement and romance, of new friends and dramatic new experiences. But Madeleine knew that such fantasies were not always fulfilled by the reality.

More importantly, the numbness that filled whole

parts of her, and that was the only way she had been able to cope with her father's death and the death of Jean, the stepmother who had filled her dead mother's place for over sixteen years, now seemed to sap the energy she needed to make the change.

She looked around her room. It was neat and tidy but too crowded with possessions. Suitcases and boxes were stacked to the ceiling above the built-in wardrobe, and the space beneath the bed was likewise full. There were so many things belonging to her parents or reminding her of her life in their comfortable old house that she could not bear to part with after the house was sold. All this would have to be sorted through again and stored.

No, she could not face it. Better to stay here where each day could be certain to be more or less the same. Dr Brownrigg had said that she would be doing this un-known Dr Galantière a favour by accepting the job, but surely if she did not, he could find someone through an agency without too much trouble?

Madeleine raised her head, feeling that her decision was made, and looked out of the window, which com-manded a view of the large hospital car-park. Several people were walking to or from it, as afternoon visiting hours were liberal, so people did not arrive and depart all in a rush. Amongst the visitors, Madeleine caught sight of a redhaired figure, and her heart gave a great lurch. The woman's walk and silhouette were so like that of Jean, and even the bright hair, caught at that moment by a strong shaft of spring sunshine, bounced about as she walked in exactly the same way.

Jean had been so vibrant, and so wise about life. She had given so much, both to Madeleine and to her father.

Madeleine remembered a day late last summer when

they had been in the garden together talking, and suddenly some words that Jean had spoken then came back to her in full force.

'You have to go out and meet life. It won't come to you. You have to be hungry for new experiences, look for them, then enjoy them with every part of you. And if bad things happen, which they will, be thankful for what you can learn from them. But don't be afraid of the bad things before they happen, or you'll hide from them and miss out on the good things too.'

For the first time in months, Madeleine found that she could cry, and that tears, instead of being the agony they had been six months ago, were a relief. When all her tears were spent, after a long time in which she simply sobbed, she lay on her bed quietly hugging the tear-dampened pillow to her, and knew that something very important had changed inside her.

'I haven't really been thinking of Father and Jean at all,' she whispered to herself. 'I suppose I haven't been able to, but now at last I can, and I can see that I haven't been doing what they would want at all. They'd have hated to see me the way I've been lately. They would want me to take this job—not because of the glamour of it but because I *do* need to see and experience more in my life.'

That night she felt more truly at peace than she had for six months, and the next afternoon she told Dr Brownrigg that she would see Christian Galantière.

Madeleine found the bustle and noise of London stimulating and exciting as she left Charing Cross station and walked along the busy sunlit streets on Thursday morning. After the flooding release of her suppressed feelings on Monday, she felt that, like some plant, she was coming alive after the long sleep of winter and slowly and tentatively putting out new growth.

She had forgotten how much she could enjoy London. Looking about, she could see office buildings with their aura of important financial activity, some people hurrying anxiously about their affairs, and others clearly enjoying the new touches of spring and colour in the air. There were shop windows gay with new season's fashions, too, and Madeleine suddenly felt dissatisfied with her own appearance. The dark blue dress she wore was neat and clean, and the white shoes and bag she carried were quite adequate, but she wished she was wearing something that celebrated the new season and the new far healthier way she was feeling.

She looked at her watch. The interview with Dr Galantière was not until half past twelve, and it was now only a quarter to ten. She had deliberately come up early, not quite sure what she intended doing with the time, but determined to spend it enjoyably. Now it was quite clear: she would buy a new dress. The boutiques of Oxford Street beckoned deliciously, and Madeleine realised that it was the first time in months that she had felt any interest at all in her appearance.

An hour later she emerged from a shop carrying two expensive parcels and wearing a third purchase—a full-skirted sundress with lightweight matching jacket in a swirling pastel pattern of flowers. Her old dress was folded into a carry-bag, and Madeleine had already decided that she would never wear it again.

But glancing at herself in a big shop-front panel of reflecting glass, she still felt that something was wrong. It was her face. Although beginning to return to its former liveliness, it still bore unmistakable signs of restless nights and frowns of tension. In the past, her cheeks had been naturally pink, matching firm, delicately moulded lips, and the clear matt of her skin and bright eyes fringed with satin lashes had needed little artificial enhancement.

Life's recent dreariness had taken its toll, however, and she was afraid that Dr Galantière might think she did not look healthy. Would he reject her for that reason? It was possible.

'Try some of our new colours,' the well-groomed sales assistant prompted as Madeleine hovered over a bewildering array of lipsticks in the cosmetics section of a large chemists a few minutes later.

'These ones here?' Madeleine asked, pointing to one rack of the display. The different shades were all very strong, but perhaps that was what she needed to give her face some colour.

'Yes. Would you like me to make up your face with some things that are a little bit new?' the assistant offered. 'See how you like it, then choose what you want to buy. It won't take long.'

Madeleine looked at her watch and decided that there was enough time. The assistant seemed very friendly, and it might be nice to try on a different image— especially if it would make her look better for the interview ahead.

She sat down on a padded stool and relaxed as the saleswoman worked over her face, giving it a complete treatment with moisturiser, foundation and blusher as well as eyeshadow, a thick coating of mascara and a glossy application of bright orchid pink lipstick. Finally, Madeleine agreed to try nail polish in a matching shade, thinking that she could remove it easily enough if she didn't like it.

But the exercise took much longer than she had

expected, and when it was finished she was horrified to find that it was already after twelve. She would be lucky to reach the French surgeon's hotel by half past, even if she took a taxi.

'What do you think?' asked the sales assistant, holding up a mirror for Madeleine to survey the result.

She gave her reflection a brief glance and did not stop to worry about the fact that she looked far more vampish and highly-coloured than she had expected.

'It's terrific,' she said quickly. 'I'll have the things you've used, then . . .'

'Oh! All right.' The girl seemed taken aback at Madeleine's quick decision. 'Anything else? Some more shades of lipgloss?'

'Oh, yes, perhaps a couple more,' Madeleine agreed quickly. 'I'm afraid I'm running rather late, though, so I haven't really got time to choose carefully.'

She picked out a blackberry-tinted shade and a more conventional red, then stood trying to conceal her impatience and anxiety as the saleswoman wrapped the purchases and added the prices painstakingly on the new computerised cash register.

Outside, feeling very weighted down by her increased collection of parcels, Madeleine stood miserably for several minutes before she managed to hail a taxi. She was only too aware of the minutes ticking relentlessly by, and when at last she climbed out of the taxi at the door of the French surgeon's hotel, paid the driver and struggled again with her parcels, it was almost a quarter to one.

Dr Galantière would be furious, of course, no matter what kind of a man he turned out to be. Madeleine realised that since Dr Brownrigg's surprise suggestion on Monday, she had not had time to put together any impression in her mind of what the unknown Frenchman would be like. As she crossed the plush-carpeted floor of the quiet foyer, after murmuring a brief explanation of her visit to one of the uniformed doormen, she wondered about the French surgeon for the first time.

Dr Brownrigg had spoken of him as a friend, so they were probably about the same age—somewhere in their early fifties. Madeleine knew also that he was 'very capable', but of course anyone in his position would be. Beyond that, he could be like any of the many surgeons she had encountered in her work.

There was only one thing that was certain, she thought nervously. He would be very angry that she was late!

He was. Pacing the spacious sitting room of his two-roomed suite, and glancing frequently at his watch, Dr Galantière felt his impatience and annoyance mounting by the second. If only he had something with which to occupy the time! But he had left the briefcase containing all his papers, as well as the paperback with which he occupied his few spare moments, with an attendant in the cloakroom of the conference area.

In the end he settled in a moody pose at the window and looked abstractedly down on to the street.

He thought back on Saturday night's formal dinner— the official opening of the conference, and staged at this top-class London hotel where most of the international delegates were staying. He had not seen Thomas Brownrigg for almost five years, and in that time he had advanced dramatically in his profession, to the point where now, in his mid-thirties, he could take three weeks paid leave to come to this important conference and deliver a paper at one of its sessions.

The two men had found themselves sitting together at one of the long tables purely by chance, but had very much enjoyed renewing their friendship and exchanging

information about their work. It was this that had led
Christian to mention his current staffing problem, and it
was then that Thomas Brownrigg had mentioned this girl
Madeleine Carver.

'She's the daughter of . . . friends of mine,' Thomas
had told him. 'She's a nurse at St Catherine's, and
although I've never worked with her myself, I'm sure
she's good. Would she be able to fill one of your vacant
positions?'

'Possibly,' Christian had replied guardedly.

He thought of the problems he had had with his last
English nurse—how she had manifestly been interested
chiefly in the night-life of the Côte d'Azur, and the
attention paid to her by rich patients. When she had
resigned just a few days before he left for England he
was only too pleased to be rid of her, even though the
fact that it coincided with a number of other departures
left him with an acute staff shortage and a lot of last-
minute work juggling staffing arrangements and finding
replacements.

Probably Sister Wallis had been one in a thousand,
but once bitten, twice shy . . . He was suspicious now of
nurses who would drop everything to come to the Côte
d'Azur, and he didn't want another nurse who was
dazzled and distracted by the undeniable glamour of the
place.

'Why do you think that your Sister Carver will want
the position?' Christian asked after a pause.

'She's had rather a difficult time lately. I don't want to
go into details—she would probably rather I didn't. I'm
worried about how run-down she seems, and I think the
change may be what she needs,' Dr Brownrigg had
explained. The English surgeon had obviously registered
Christian's hesitation, as his next words were spoken

very seriously. 'I don't often ask favours, Christian, but I'd very much like you to take this girl on. I'm sure you'd be happy with her.'

At that point Christian had agreed to arrange an interview. After all, it was very likely that the prejudice he had formed was unjustifiable. In addition, Thomas Brownrigg had done a lot for him in the past—during those two years at the London hospital which had seemed so alien at first, when his English had been far less fluent than he had wanted, and when one or two of the staff had been openly hostile to a foreigner in their midst. It was a simple favour, and it would have been churlish and against his nature to refuse—although now, looking at his expensive streamlined watch again and noting that it was almost a quarter to one, Christian began to wish that he had.

He frowned, sighed noisily between clenched teeth and resumed his survey of the street two floors below. A taxi had just pulled up outside the hotel entrance, disgorging a young woman whom Christian judged to be in her early twenties. She was clutching a number of untidy-looking parcels and her hair was slightly disarrayed, although as she looked up briefly, Christian saw that she was carefully and heavily made up—too heavily for his taste.

He also noticed the worried frown that creased her forehead, and the anxious way in which she consulted her wrist-watch. Good God! This couldn't be Sister Carver, could it?

Madeleine wondered if all hotel lifts were as slow as this one seemed to be. Dr Galantière's room was only two floors up, but with every second of lateness that accumulated, the impression she was making on the Frenchman would be worsening. It was horrible, too, to have to stare at herself in the mirrors that covered all four sides of the lift.

Under the glare of harsh fluorescent lighting, her face looked positively lurid, though she guessed that for night-time wear the skilled application might look quite attractive. It was definitely not the face that became a sensible nurse at a job interview, however, not to mention the fingernails which showed to full effect against the white paper of the parcels she was carrying.

The doors slid open at last and Madeleine found Number 207 only a little way down the corridor. She stood there for a moment trying to compose herself, but suddenly, before she could knock, the door had been opened by the swift movement of an impatient hand and she was confronted by a man utterly unlike the hazy picture she had begun to form.

For one thing, he was far younger—somewhere in his thirties, she guessed. He was far darker, too, than many Frenchmen, with thick black hair that fell in wayward curls which would make almost any woman long to pass caressing hands through them. His eyes were black, too, and shone now with the cold light of anger. His lean but powerful frame beneath the crisply cut suit of pale grey was taut with impatience.

'Are you . . . Dr Christian Galantière?' she stammered—stupidly, because of course he was, even if he did not look like any other doctor she had ever met.

'Yes, and I presume you are Madeleine Carver?' His English was fluent and only slightly accented, and his voice was richly-timbred, though steely now.

'Yes, and I'm so terribly sorry to be late. I'm not from London, and I underestimated how long it would take to . . .'

'Let's not waste any more time, then, shall we?' His

reply cut smoothly across her own gabbled words, and he led her to a fat, crimson-velvet-upholstered easy chair as he spoke, taking its twin for himself.

He did not offer to send for anything to drink, but then perhaps it was not to be expected that he would. After all, her lateness was inexcusable. He might well have another appointment to go to, and Madeleine was bitterly aware that the bad impression he already seemed to have formed was in every way quite justified.

'May I see your references and work reports, and so forth?' he asked immediately. 'I presume you have brought them with you . . . ?'

'Oh . . . yes, they're here somewhere.'

Madeleine bit her lip. How stupid! She had slid the folder of neatly-ordered papers into one of her shopping bags for convenience, intending to get it out and have it ready before seeing him, but in her anxiety about being late, it had slipped her mind. Now, of course, she had no idea which of the three bags it was in, and had to search through each one. She was conscious, as she fumbled in the taped-up bags, of those lurid fingernails, and of Dr Galantière staring sardonically at them. Would he notice that under the opaque pink they were neatly clipped as a nurse's nails should be?

Probably not.

She handed the folder over silently, after finding it in the last of the bags, then sat there rigidly while he examined its contents, unable to relax into the seductive comfort of the chair as she would have liked to do.

'This seems quite satisfactory,' he said briefly after a few moments. '*Et vous parlez français?*'

He shot the question at her without warning.

'Yes, I speak French,' Madeleine replied in that language, stumbling a little over the rolled 'r's, but not too flustered. She guessed that this was to be a quick test of her fluency, so she continued in French to talk about her A level studies, her two holidays in Brittany, and the school trip to Paris.

When she had finished, she waited for him to say something in praise of her efforts, as she did feel she had spoken quite fluently, but he merely nodded meditatively a few times.

'Now tell me, why are you interested in this job?' He spoke in English again now.

He was observing her narrowly and disconcertingly, his black eyes unreadable. Madeleine thought of the struggle it had been to keep going through the last six months, then of Monday's revelation and emotion, and her new feeling that both her father and Jean would want her to take this step. Could she say anything about these things to the man who sat opposite watching her so coldly?

It seemed impossible.

For a moment she struggled against a lump that had formed in her throat, then made the only reply she could manage—a very light one.

'Who wouldn't want a job in the South of France?'

It was even accompanied by a gay laugh that rang insincerely in her own ears. What would he think? It did not matter. Her lateness and nervousness had cost her the job by now, in any case . . .

'An interesting answer.' One side of his mouth curved upwards in a faint and rather cynical smile, but he did not probe further, to her relief. Instead, both of them sat there in silence for what seemed like minutes to Madeleine.

During that time, Christian was thinking very hard. It would scarcely have been possible for someone to make a worse first impression on him than this nurse had done. Fifteen minutes late, made up like an actress in a night-club, and clutching all those untidy parcels. She had obviously been unable to resist shopping for one last thing at the end of this morning's spree. That was the real reason for her lateness, and she had lied about it to save face. Then there had been that flippant and shallow reply to his last question.

What had Thomas Brownrigg said about her? That she had had 'a rather difficult time lately,' and the change would be good for her. Probably Thomas was being too soft. The girl had had trouble with a boy-friend, or perhaps she had been involved in some kind of romantic scandal at the hospital. An affair with a mar-ried doctor? That would fit with the type of personality which she seemed to represent. After his recent experi-ence with Sister Wallis, his instinct was to refuse Madeleine Carver the job and go to an agency, but Thomas would be very disappointed, and possibly angry. Going to an agency would take time, and he did owe Thomas a favour . . . Christian Galantière suppressed a sigh.

'The job is yours,' he said, breaking the long silence.

'I beg your pardon?' Madeleine stammered. She had become quite certain by now that she had no chance.

'I said that the job is yours. What's the matter? Don't you really want it?'

'I . . . Of course I do, it's just that . . .'

'You thought that by being fifteen minutes late you had . . . er . . . blown your chances?' He pronounced the idiom carefully and with a strong note of sarcasm.

'Yes.' He had read her mind too clearly.

'I'm glad you realise that some people place a certain weight on punctuality, then, even though it does not seem to be a virtue you practise yourself,' he drawled, one well-drawn eyebrow raised.

Madeleine could think of no reply. Protestations that she had not once been late for work by so much as a minute during her four years of training and working at St Catherine's Hospital would no doubt be received with scepticism. All she could do was determine to prove herself in the future when they were working together.

Working together! It suddenly struck her that she would have to see a lot more of this disturbing man, whose antagonism she had succeeded in arousing so thoroughly. For a moment she wished wholeheartedly that he had refused to employ her.

'However,' he was continuing now after a pause, 'when you work with us at Le Breuil you will be punctual to the minute, or you will not last long in that South of France which you seem to find so glamorous—and I had better mention that we do have rules about nails and make-up in our hospital as well.'

'Yes, Dr Galantière.'

'And now I am afraid you must leave,' he said, rising to his feet as he spoke, in one easy, economical movement.

He certainly was not anxious to prolong the conversation, Madeleine thought grimly. And he had given her no chance to ask any of the many questions she had concerning the work and the hospital. Obviously he was a very busy man—and that was probably the only reason he had accepted her for the job in the first place.

As for that comment about nails and make-up! Need he be quite so cold and arrogant in the way he expressed himself?

'I have to return to the conference,' he was saying now. 'I'll be in touch with you about the details of your employment, but how soon before you will be able to leave St Catherine's?'

'I should give two weeks' notice.'

'Good. I return to Le Breuil in two weeks. We shall travel down there together in my car—not, perhaps, an ideal arrangement for either of us, but you will agree that it is convenient?'

'Yes, I suppose it is.' She made her tone as expressionless as she could.

'I shall, of course, endeavour to make the trip as enjoyable as I can for you,' he said smoothly, and then, following that startling comment, and without another word, he had ushered her out of the door and closed it behind her.

It was not an auspicious start to this new phase of her life. By the time Madeleine reached the lift, she had decided that she was not going to like Dr Christian Galantière one bit.

CHAPTER TWO

THE French surgeon's streamlined cream MG was
already speeding through the English countryside as the
sun's early rays shone through the spring greenery,
transforming it into a lacework of translucent colours.

Madeleine had not slept well the night before, always
conscious through her restless tossing and turnings of the
fact that she had to rise at five in order to be well
and truly ready when the doctor called for her at the
Brownriggs' house at six. But she felt wide awake now
in spite of her bad night, too tense and too aware of
the man at her side to relax and enjoy the scenery, or
doze.

The two weeks since her interview with the disturbing
Frenchman had passed incredibly quickly. First thing
the next morning she had written out her notice and
handed it in, to be greeted by surprised and disappointed
exclamations from the Director of Nursing, Sister
Malvern, and then her best wishes for the new life that
lay ahead.

Then had come the task of packing her things, made
much easier by the Brownriggs' offer to store everything
that she did not need in their clean, roomy cellar.
Friends had to be told, in person, by phone or by mail,
and farewells made to everyone with whom she had
worked at the hospital.

Madeleine had also bought herself a French diction-
ary, a reference grammar, and a refresher course textbook, and had found time to write out a few lists of

nursing terms in French to learn during every spare moment.

She had not seen or spoken to Christian Galantière again until this morning. He had made all the arrangements through Dr Brownrigg, and it had been decided that, after a quiet afternoon tea party given for her by her closest friends among the nurses, she would spend her last night in England at the Brownriggs' cheerful house. Madeleine had made her own breakfast and brought her luggage downstairs to the front hall, then Dr and Mrs Brownrigg had woken and dressed just in time to say goodbye as Christian Galantière drove up to the house.

'You'll write, won't you?' Barbara had whispered, giving Madeleine a final hug while her husband and Dr Galantière exchanged greetings, then Madeleine's one modest suitcase had been loaded into the back of the car and they were on their way.

'You haven't brought much luggage,' was Dr Galantière's first comment as he headed for the highway, making complicated turns without seeming to need either Madeleine's help, or that of a road map.

'No, not much,' Madeleine agreed briefly.

She wasn't going to explain that the task of sorting through all her possessions had been too much for her, so she had simply packed those items that were in constant daily use, as well as her French books and the three new dresses she had brought during that ill-fated shopping spree two weeks ago. Let him assume that she was planning to restock her wardrobe with expensive items from the shops in Cannes and Nice! He obviously thought she was fashion-mad and disapproved of it.

After this short exchange, silence had fallen and was still unbroken. Every now and then Madeleine ventured a glance at the smoothly-chiselled profile of the surgeon, but he seemed absorbed in driving and in following some train of thought which she could only guess at. Probably it concerned his work. After all, he had been away for three weeks, and Madeleine guessed that he was a man who liked to feel completely in control. Doubtless, he would have learnt things at the conference that he was anxious to put into practice, and was already beginning to think of how he would do it.

'There is a cushion and a rug on the back seat,' he said suddenly, breaking her train of musings. 'Use them if you feel like a sleep.'

'Thank you, I will,' Madeleine replied, and reached over for them.

She was still not in the least sleepy, but if she pretended to be, the silence between them would not seem so awkward and she would feel free to let her thoughts roam where they pleased.

Half an hour later the cosy warmth of the cream mohair rug and the inviting plumpness of the matching silk-covered cushion had lulled her into a doze.

'Miss Carver . . .' Dr Galantière's hand was surprisingly soft on her shoulder, and his voice was lowered gently when he woke her some time later. 'We're at the boat.'

Madeleine stretched and blinked confusedly for a few moments, then looked ahead. They had slowed to a crawl now, as officials directed them into the approach to the cross-channel ferry.

'You know, you look quite different when you are asleep,' Dr Galantière told her, smiling to reveal startlingly white teeth.

Madeleine searched for a reply but could find none, and was very glad when a uniformed man approached and the French surgeon wound down his window to speak to him. Minutes later they had left the car and were on their way to the passenger deck of the ship.

It was odd and disturbing to be walking beside this near-stranger, Madeleine thought, taking stock again of his well-proportioned height, his thick black hair, the easy grace with which he moved and the well-fitting clothes he wore. Last time she had seen him, he was in a suit, but today he had chosen something more casual—blue canvas jeans and a silver-grey shirt—slightly open around his bronzed neck, and covered by a lightweight jacket in darker grey.

By pure coincidence, the outfit exactly complemented Madeleine's own blue skirt with its subtle textured stripe, and her lacy-collared white blouse and fluffy full-sleeved angora pullover of pearl grey. Everyone would automatically assume them to be a couple—married or engaged, and setting off on some romantic Continental holiday.

'Where would you like to sit?' the surgeon asked.

They had arrived in the main passenger area now, and he had turned to her to ask the question, his sleeve brushing her hand slightly as he did so.

'Up the front, please, if that's all right with you. I'd enjoy watching our progress,' she replied, trying to sound casual.

She was tempted to move away from him, to make it clear to the other passengers that they were work associates, not a married couple, but she did not know why it seemed important that their relationship should be clear. Madeleine realised that she knew nothing of the French surgeon's personal life. He had been alone in England, but that meant nothing. There could very easily be a wife waiting for him at Le Breuil—No, wait a minute. Hadn't Barbara said something about him being a bachelor last night at supper? Yes, she remembered now.

That did not mean that there was no woman—or women—in his life, of course. Madeleine guessed that there would be many women who would be very happy to be seen in the company of a man like Christian Galantière. Undeniably he had charms—although she reminded herself that she was impervious to them. After the bad footing they had begun on, it seemed quite impossible that they should ever become friends, let alone anything more.

'Would you like something to eat and drink?' he asked now, interrupting her train of thought. They had chosen seats very near to the front windows of the passenger lounge and Madeleine saw that behind them was a bar.

'Just an orange juice, thank you,' she replied to his question.

'Nothing to eat?'

'No, I had quite a good breakfast.'

Dr Galantière left her and went in search of the drinks. He was certainly being quite adequate and pleasant in his attentions today, she thought, but it did not mean that his real opinion of her had changed at all, and perversely, she decided that she did not care. She was confident that she would be able to prove her worth as a nurse once she began work at Le Breuil, and it was likely that, hospital hierarchies being what they were, she would not see very much of him there—certainly not socially, anyway.

Madeleine thought again of her father and Jean, and her reasons for deciding to make the change and go to France. At Le Breuil she wanted to experience as much as possible, explore new surroundings, and meet many new people, recover her old joy in life. Dr Christian Galantière was really a very incidental figure in all this.

He came back quite soon with her orange juice, as well as a mineral water for himself, and the boat journey passed as the car journey through the south of England had done—largely in silence. Dr Galantière took from his briefcase the thick paper-bound volume of transcripts from the medical conference and studied it with pencil in hand, making notes in the margin.

Madeleine very much wished she had thought to put one of the French books in her bag, instead of locking them in the suitcase which was now in the doctor's car. With her she had only the paperback novel she was reading, and she hoped Dr Galantière would not notice it and comment sardonically upon its frivolity.

But he did not glance her way even once, and by the end of the trip she decided that he had virtually forgotten her existence.

It was quite late when they were again seated in the sporty little left-hand-drive MG, and Madeleine was hungry. The taciturn Frenchman had not mentioned lunch, but when they reached the town of St Omer he detoured through some side streets, then pulled up smoothly outside a pleasant-looking restaurant.

'We'll eat here. You must be hungry.'

'Yes, I am,' she admitted, and followed him gratefully into the dim friendly-looking interior.

It was good to be in France again. Madeleine had loved all three of her visits here. Her French teacher had known how to show her students Paris at its best, and Father and Jean had always favoured adventurous, interest-filled excursions to all manner of local sights. Neither had they stinted themselves in their explorations of local cuisine, and some mouthwatering memories of meals she had eaten with them came back to Madeleine.

Strangely, though, she could begin to think of these things now without the biting slice of pain running through her that she had become used to. The memories had a poignant sadness which they would never lose, but they were memories she wanted to keep and enjoy.

For the meal they both chose a light *consommé* followed by a country-style *ragoût* that was accompanied by green salad and crisp, golden-crusted bread.

'You may have wine,' Christian told her, 'but I will not, as I am driving.'

He spoke civilly but not warmly, and Madeleine wondered whether they would find anything to talk to each other about during the meal.

'No, no wine for me, either,' she said. 'Are you having mineral water?'

'Yes.'

'Then I'll have some too.'

There was silence, as Madeleine had feared there would be, during the first part of the meal, but as she sat there idly noting the long brown surgeon's fingers that gripped Dr Galantière's cold glass, she was reminded of the work they would soon be involved in together, and remembered that there were still many questions she wanted to ask about Le Breuil.

'Please tell me more about the hospital while we're sitting here,' she begged impulsively. 'I'm so looking forward to seeing it, as I trained at St Catherine's, and have seen so little of how medicine works in other places.'

Christian Galantière looked up sharply from his plate at her words, as if he distrusted the enthusiasm of her tone. Probably he *did* distrust it, Madeleine reflected, with the bad impression he had formed of her personality still in his mind. After his initial pause, he replied quite reasonably, though, and they were drinking their coffee before had finished answering her questions in an interesting way that revealed his enthusiasm for his profession.

'We had better not linger,' he said after they had drained the last drops of their bitter, aromatic brew.

As they walked out together, Madeleine was conscious again of how like a couple they must seem. He was very close to her as they passed through the low door of the restaurant, and she was suddenly aware of the fact—aware of the faint scent of musk and maleness that hovered about him, and aware of the deliciously smooth look of the brown skin in the curve between his neck and his shoulder.

'Would you like me to take a turn at driving?' she asked him suddenly, to distract her thoughts from the dangerous turn they had taken.

He looked at her coolly with his dark head tilted slightly to one side, his hand paused on the handle of the car door. Madeleine was sure he was going to refuse.

'I don't often let people drive this car,' he said. 'It's rather precious to me. But yes. It's a long journey and it's dangerous for me to do it all. Obviously you have a valid licence?'

'Yes, and I've driven in France once before.'

'From now until we reach Paris, then? We will be on the autoroute soon, and it will be very easy.'

Madeleine took the driving seat and after he had given clear, concise instructions about the management of gears, indicators, and one or two other things, they were away. She thoroughly enjoyed her session at the wheel. Although the soft collapsible top of the car was up at the moment, windows provided access to the fresh invigorating air of a French spring afternoon. The feeling of controlled speed was exhilarating, and although Madeleine could not concentrate on the scenery, she could at least glimpse it and begin to have her appetite whetted again for tiny crookedly piled up villages, decorated churches and curiously designed farmsteads, as well as the greenery that lay between them.

The modern architecture of petrol service stations and factories was less attractive, of course, but it was all part of France, and all, on this sunny afternoon, full of promise.

She was quite sorry when Dr Galantière suggested that she pull over for him to take the wheel again as they entered the outskirts of the great city.

'Will we be driving through the heart of Paris?' she asked a few minutes later.

'I'm afraid not. It's much quicker to go around the *périphérique* and rejoin the autoroute,' Dr Galantière replied. 'You're disappointed, of course. But there would not have been time for you to stop and shop in any case.'

The tone was superficially a mild one.

'Oh, really—how ridiculous! I only meant . . .'

'I was under the impression that you rather liked shopping.' His faintly accented but again mild reply cut off her outburst.

'Well, I do, sometimes, Madeleine agreed, making her voice very reasonable as his was. 'But it's not one of my principal concerns in life, whatever you may believe. I'm disappointed about not seeing the city because I visited Paris once before, as I think I told you, and loved it. That was in autumn, and I was hoping to catch a glimpse of it now in spring. But I quite see that it would add a lot of time to our journey.'

'You'll see it again another time, perhaps,' was all that the Frenchman replied.

Madeleine wondered how long it would turn out to be before she passed through the famous city again. She might be settled in France for several years if she liked it at Le Breuil, but of course there would be holidays in which she would return to England, and pass through Paris . . .

It was late afternoon when Dr Galantière turned off the autoroute again.

'Where are we going? May I see a map?' Madeleine asked curiously. She always took an interest in tracing the route during a long drive.

'You may of course look at a map, but we will be arriving very soon, so there is really no need,' he replied, coolly as ever.

'Arriving? But I thought . . .'

'We are spending the night at Fontainebleau.'

This came as a complete shock. Somehow, in all the planning of arrangements and details, neither Christian Galantière nor Dr Brownrigg had mentioned that there would be an overnight break in the journey, and Madeleine had assumed that the busy surgeon was planning to drive through the night, to arrive at some time in the early hours of the morning.

Madeleine's heart sank at the prospect of the journey being prolonged. They would have to have two more meals together than she had thought, and for politeness' sake, spend at least part of the evening in each other's company. As well, she had been counting on travelling much of the way at night, when she would have been able to lie back and doze, and forget about Dr Galantière at her side. Now there would be the necessity of making conversation with the man again tomorrow.

They had entered the outskirts of the town now, and the surgeon was speaking again. Thank goodness he did not seem to have noticed her reaction to his last announcement!

'It's still quite early,' he was saying casually. 'We can check in at the hotel and have coffee, then you will be able to look at the gardens of the Château, if such things interest you.'

'That would be lovely!' Madeleine replied with sincere enthusiasm, her blue eyes lighting up and neutralising the shadows that still lay beneath them. She ignored the slight sarcasm that had underlain his last words.

'What about the Château itself? Perhaps that's not open to tourists?'

'It is, but we will be a little too late, I'm afraid,' he said, not reacting noticeably to her enlivened face.

Madeleine decided with a little spurt of anger that he distrusted her to the extent of not even believing that her enthusiasm was real. Did he think she was feigning it to prove something to him about her interest in things other than the frivolities of clothes and make-up? Well, he was wrong, and she was beginning to feel that the antagonism—veiled though it was—that emanated towards her from him was going beyond a joke. It was as if he was testing her every response for evidence of her shallowness.

'I'm simply not going to play up to it,' she decided. 'It *was* wrong and silly of me to be late for the interview that day—I should have guessed that the girl would take longer over my face than she said—but Dr Galantière has agreed to take me on, so he should at least act as if he trusts me. I don't really think I respect someone who can be so judgmental.'

It felt good, in a perverse kind of way, to have reached this decision about the man, to have decided to feel quite as coolly about him as he did about her. Now she could turn her attention to the delightful hotel outside which Dr Galantière had just stopped his car.

It was an old building, but immaculately kept and in keeping with the architecture in the rest of the street. When Madeleine entered the foyer at Dr Galantière's side she found it cool and pleasant with its thick carpet and quiet atmosphere. At the reception desk, Madeleine did not miss the glance of surprise that the slim, efficient-looking receptionist gave herself and Dr Galantière when the surgeon said that two single rooms had been booked in his name.

'She can't make us out at all,' Madeleine mused. 'I suppose it might be a little unusual.'

'Our rooms are side by side,' Christian murmured in his rich, slightly-accented voice as they were led up a flight of carpeted stairs. 'I hope you don't mind.'

'Not unless you snore *very* loudly,' Madeleine replied blandly. 'Why should I mind?'

'Some people would. They would read some hidden meaning into the thing.'

The surgeon shrugged as he said this—an expressive movement, as his shoulders were very powerful—and glanced at her. His face was quite immobile—No, it wasn't. Madeleine amended her observation quickly and with satisfaction. Unmistakably, the corners of his mouth were twitching in a smile that he was trying unsuccessfully to suppress. Her mild attempt at humour had actually got through to him!

She was pleased. There was something very satisfying about making a man laugh against his will—even if you don't like him.

At that moment they reached their rooms and the baggage boy opened the door for her.

'I'll see you downstairs for coffee in ten minutes?' Dr Galantière queried with a light questioning intonation.

'Lovely!'

'There is a very pleasant terrace at the side which should still be in the sun.'

Then he left her and went to his own room. Alone, Madeleine realised how glad she was of the chance to stretch her legs and freshen up, and it was only just within the prescribed ten minutes when she went down the stairs again and found the terrace Dr Galantière had mentioned. Not that being late was important on this occasion, but there was no sense in calling attention to the issue of punctuality again.

The terrace was charming and sunny as the surgeon had suggested, and Madeleine only wished she could be sitting there in the company of someone with whom she felt more relaxed. Approaching the white-clothed table, she watched Dr Galantière as he looked idly at the patch of garden beyond the terrace.

Even when relaxed as it was now, his body gave off the impression of lazy power beneath the well-fitting clothes. Madeleine thought of the other attributes he possessed: intelligence, success, taste, and—in all probability—a certain degree of wealth as well. From the brief conversations they had exchanged, Madeleine could guess that he would be very able either to speak seriously and intelligently to a companion, or to be amusing and lively in his talk. Probably also, that deep voice could be used tenderly and caressingly. There would be many women who would find all this very attractive.

And his smile too. She caught a brief glimpse of it as

she sat down opposite him, and was startled by the softened, mischievous look it gave to his face.

'I've ordered coffee. That was what you wanted?'

'Yes, thank you. I'm looking forward to it.'

'And they'll bring a trolley of cakes for us to choose from as well.'

Everything came a few minutes later, and Madeleine chose a gooey chocolate custard-filled choux puff to complement the strength of the coffee. Christian had a less flamboyant lemon tart. They ate in silence, but this was starting to seem less awkward now—probably because Madeleine was getting used to it. She let her thoughts wander and was recalled only when the dark surgeon put down his empty white cup and spoke.

'I must go and work now,' he said. 'You should go and look at the grounds of the Château if you want to see them, or you will run out of time. We shall have dinner fairly early, if that suits you. At seven o'clock.'

'Of course. I'm happy to do whatever you suggest.'

As she gathered up her bag and jacket she saw the waiter noting down the price of the things they had eaten, and a thought occurred to her.

'How are my expenses on his journey being covered?'

He turned to her, frowning for a moment as if his thoughts had been far away, then his brow cleared.

'Don't worry about that. Partly they are covered by the terms of your employment. The rest will be subtracted from your first pay. I trust that is not inconvenient?'

'Not at all.'

Madeleine saw that the surgeon's head had already turned away again towards the garden. Obviously he had been involved in thinking about his work and her query had been an annoying distraction. She was sorry that she had not timed it better and felt flustered and ill at ease for the first few minutes of her walk to the Château. She regretted more and more the circumstances that had allowed her to make such a bad impression on him that day two weeks ago. It meant she was now so conscious of every awkwardness that happened, every sign of disapproval and irritation in him. Memories of their first encounter played over and over in her mind and became more exaggerated the more she thought of them. It was silly, but she could not seem to help it.

It would be even sillier, though, to let it spoil the rest of this sunny afternoon, she decided firmly, switching her attention to the picturesque buildings she was passing, and the panorama of the Château with its formal grounds. The hour-long exploration was a delightful one. In spite of the intruding presence of other tourists, Madeleine became lost in the atmosphere of the past as she imagined the glittering figures who must have strolled these walks at one time.

A pamphlet told her that several kings of the old régime had lived or been born here, and that Napoleon had abdicated his throne here in 1814. The tranquillity of the carp pond and the canal were more than pleasant, too.

It was six by the time she reached her room again, and the private bathroom beckoned invitingly. Only silence issued from next door. Madeleine assumed that Christian was still hard at work over his conference papers.

She luxuriated in the hot clean water of the bath for nearly half an hour, then dressed with care in one of the dresses she had recently bought—a deep smoky pink cheesecloth that was almost plum; it fell from a broderie anglaise bodice, and narrow shoulder straps left her smooth pale shoulders bare.

Madeleine had tormented herself for several minutes in the bath as she tried to decide what dress would be best. It would not do to seem too casual, but neither did she want him to think that fashion was an obsession with her. The problem was solved when she looked into her suitcase and found that, being made of crinkly cheese-cloth, the plummy pink dress was the only suitable garment that was not creased.

Make-up was the next problem, of course. She sat perplexed in front of the mirror, then with sudden resolution, spoke her thoughts aloud.

'I'll wear what I feel like wearing, and I'll look as I feel happy looking.'

She touched her lashes with mascara, relieved the pallor of her cheeks with a light dusting of blusher and chose a neutral but glossy lipstick, then decided she was satisfied. Dressing to please a man—especially one she did not even like!—was both demeaning and dangerous.

'Very nice,' was his murmured comment, after she had answered his tap at her door a while later.

'Then we're well matched,' she replied in kind, privately cursing cheesecloth, because as before, the way that their clothes complemented each other was quite uncanny.

He wore a dark suit in a modern cut—conventional enough, but the thin stripes that ran through the white shirt beneath, and the colour of his silk tie, were of exactly the same muted deep pink as her own dress.

Then as they walked into the restaurant together, a middle-aged Englishman, who obviously assumed that everyone around him spoke only French, commented quite loudly to his wife: 'What a striking-looking couple!' Madeleine flushed, turned her head and pretended to be studying a landscape painting on the wall, refusing the catch Christian Galantière's eye or respond to his low sardonic chuckle.

'Perhaps you had better tell me tonight what you are planning to wear tomorrow,' he murmured to her as they took their seats.

So he had noticed how their clothing matched too! But she could not help responding with a smile and saw an answering twinkle in his own eyes when she replied: 'I'll let you know later.'

Their eyes met for an uncomfortable few seconds, and it was a relief to be able to take refuge from his gaze by consulting the menu which had been brought promptly to their table.

It was a delicious meal—seafood cocktail in a piquant sauce followed by tender chicken breasts and mushroom pâté wrapped in feathery pastry. And the crisp white wine that Christian Galantière chose from the wide range softened and relaxed Madeleine so that she almost forgot the reasons she had for feeling awkward with the French surgeon.

She had guessed earlier that he might be a charming companion, and tonight he was. His smile came frequently as he talked, and was very white against the heavy natural tan of his skin. As for his eyes, they were just black pools in the dim light.

Madeleine did not realise it, but she herself was at her best tonight. The shadows beneath her eyes were beginning to disappear now, and a sense of adventure and new experiences to come, stimulated by her exploration of the Château grounds this afternoon, was making her livelier than she had been for months. Her conversation had a sharp edge of wit and intelligence, and she was an enchanting listener as well, her deep blue eyes fixed intently on Christian as he spoke, and her lips responding with a smile to each of his teasing remarks and jests.

'I'm enjoying this too much.' The thought flashed briefly through Madeleine's mind like a danger signal, but she ignored it.

They lingered over their dessert and coffee, still chatting, then with evident regret, Dr Galantière rose to his feet.

'I really don't want to,' he said, his accent softening the words into a caress. 'But I must work on those conference papers some more while everything is still fresh in my mind. Are you coming upstairs?'

'Yes. Yes, I'll . . . do some French study, perhaps.' Madeleine stood up as well, feeling lightheaded after the two glasses of wine she had drunk and wondering if she was imagining the dramatic change in their relationship since this morning—since only a few hours ago, in fact.

She noticed that there were only two people still in the restaurant. They obviously *were* a couple, on their honeymoon probably, as they were whispering together and leaning towards each other intimately over their table in the dimmest corner of the restaurant.

The light in the corridor outside Madeleine and Christian's rooms had been turned down a little now, creating a mellow golden glow. They had walked up the stairs together in a comfortable silence, slowing as they reached her door. Madeleine got out her key, and then was not even very surprised when Christian waited for her to do so and slowly reached a hand out to her shoulder, eased her close to him and kissed her gently with warm, firm lips.

'Good night . . . I'll see you in the morning.' The

words were a caressing whisper, and Madeleine could manage only a husky 'Yes' in reply.

Then Christian touched her cheek lightly with one finger, smiled, and turned away to his own room.

Madeleine sank heavily against the inside of the door when she had entered her room. There had been a definite promise in that kiss, she was almost certain—as certain as anyone could be of anything when their head was in a whirl, their knees were weak, and everything they thought they knew about a person seemed to have crumbled and vanished in the course of a short evening.

She looked abstractedly at her watch. It was not yet even ten. What had it all meant? She badly wanted to see him, talk to him again and ask him, but of course it was out of the question. He had said good night, he wanted to work.

Madeleine remembered that she had said she would study some French. She sat down on the bed and flipped through a few pages of the refresher course textbook she had bought, absorbing little of it. Every time she thought of the brief touch of his kiss she could feel it again on her lips with a thrill of pleasure and fear. If only he had said something more!

No. What was there to say? Reason took over suddenly. It was a light flirtation, nothing more. Or if there was the possibility of something more, it could take time to develop. She would not think about it any more. She would relax and let tomorrow come. She would make her preparations for the night, then get into bed with the grammar textbook and concentrate on some work as he would be doing . . .

When she awoke the next morning to the sound of a polite tap at the door, the book had fallen to the floor. The light was off, though, and when she shook sleep away a little more she dimly remembered having reached out to the nearby switch. The night's sleep had been a very sound one—not so surprising, perhaps, after yesterday's early start and the soporific effect of the wine.

A second tap sounded at the door, so she roused herself enough to call 'Come in' in French. It would be a maid. Christian must have given instructions that she be woken in time to go down to breakfast.

But the neatly uniformed maid already carried a tray.

'Monsieur le Docteur said you would have your breakfast in bed,' she explained as Madeleine struggled to a sitting position.

'How lovely!' She was conscious of a faint disappointment that she would not see Christian . . . Dr Galantière, so soon this way, but it was a very thoughtful gesture on his part.

The maid stepped out again and shut the door behind her, while Madeleine put a spare pillow behind her back and prepared to enjoy the freshly-brewed *café-au-lait* and still-warm croissant with pale unsalted butter and strawberry jam.

It was just as she was putting the empty plate and cup back on the tray that another tap came at her door. It opened in response to her acknowledgment and this time Christian's dark head slid through, making Madeleine's heart turn strangely as she saw it.

'You've finished?' he asked. 'Good. Would you be able to be ready to leave in half an hour?'

'I think so.'

'I'll meet you in the foyer, then.'

'All right.'

He was gone again too quickly, leaving her with just one smile to show that he still felt at least some of the warmth of the night before. Madeleine got out of bed, showered and dressed quickly, then packed and closed her suitcase and was ready to leave within the stipulated time. She decided to carry the case downstairs herself rather than call a baggage boy. Christian was already waiting for her.

'I'm not late?'

'No. I'm a few minutes early. Let's get going at once.'

He was cheerful and friendly, not gentle and caressing in his manner as he had been the night before, but then it was hardly to be expected that he would be at this hour of the morning. It was now only eight o'clock. Madeleine responded to his manner in the same vein and enjoyed hearing something about the history and geography of the landscapes through which they travelled, as well as taking quite a long turn at driving the easy-handling sports car herself.

They reached Lyon shortly before lunch-time.

'Do you mind if we don't stop at a restaurant today?' Christian asked. 'I'm anxious not to get back too late. I thought we could have a picnic by the side of the road somewhere. We'll stop here in Lyon and I'll buy a few things.'

'That would be lovely,' agreed Madeleine. She enjoyed al-fresco meals just as much as eating in restaurants, and it suddenly seemed gloriously and typically French to be stopping off at a little shop to buy a long crusty stick of bread, a pat of butter, cheese, home-style brandy and herb-flavoured *pâté* and a few tomatoes, as well as fruit juice and mineral water.

The weather was sunny, and even more spring-like today than it had been yesterday now that they were getting further south. Christian produced a picnic rug from the boot of the car and turned into an interesting-

looking side road which soon came out on a hilltop
where they could sit in dappled shade and look out on a
French farm scene—animals grazing, trees bending a
little in the breeze, and spring flowers spreading a carpet
of colours in the fields.

They used their fingers unashamedly as they ate,
breaking bread, then using a knife to spread butter and
pâté and to slice the tomatoes. Christian was relaxed and
smiling, lying back as the breeze brushed a loose black
curl or two over his forehead. Madeleine was content to
talk only a little and spend the rest of the time enjoying
the food, the view and her own thoughts. She could not
help feeling happiness within her almost as a solid
physical force. It seemed so right to have come to
France. Jean and Father would want to see her like this,
smiling in the sun, instead of growing pale in the toiling
routine that took her back and forth between the
hospital and the Nurses' Residence.

She would have more picnics like this, and see much
more of France, explore thoroughly as much as she
could of the Côte d'Azur. Would Christian be with her
on these expeditions? It was too soon to think about it,
of course, but she somehow thought—and hoped—that
he might be. Wasn't this already different from anything
she had felt before? She didn't want to think that it could
be. That was too dangerous.

There had been men in her life before, of course. A
warmhearted and intelligent nurse does not go for long
without being asked out by members of staff if it is
known that she has no steady boy-friend. She had had
brief infatuations, and sometimes longer relationships
that might have progressed further, except that they
were never quite right. She had always told herself that
she had plenty of time and was not going to get serious

about the first man who showed an interest in her.

In the past six months she had not even thought this, finding it too painful to let any emotion touch her at all deeply. Wasn't she emerging from this now, though? Might not she soon be ready to be touched?

Her thoughts returned to the present and to Christian. He had leaned over to recap the unfinished bottle of mineral water, and was now lying quite close to her, looking at her with a soft smile playing around his lips.

'The sun suits you,' he said, lifting himself up on to one elbow, and reaching out a lazy hand to run it through her hair.

Madeleine felt a thrill tremble through her, and did not even hesitate when he slid his hips closer on the rug and took her in his arms. His kiss was warmer and more alive than the sunshine that bathed them, and his chest against her body was solid and supportive. The musky scent that hovered around him enveloped her and seduced her senses into willing response. When he broke away, still smiling and lazy, she felt a keen sense of loss.

'I could stay here for several more hours, I think,' Christian said. 'But of course we can't. Have you finished eating? Shall we pack up and go?'

'We'll have to.' Her voice echoed the regret in his.

They shook the crumbs out of the rug, then folded it and tidied the scraps into a paper bag which they took with them to dispose of properly later, not talking much, but completely relaxed with each other.

It was late afternoon when they had left Cannes behind them and turned up the coast towards Nice.

'Le Breuil isn't on the map,' said Madeleine, after studying it carefully.

'No, it's too small,' Christian replied. 'Just a village. It hardly has a separate existence now that the coast is becoming so built up. The hospital itself goes by the name of Le Breuil, and I confess that is what I am always thinking of when I use the name.'

'It's quite soon?'

'Yes,' he replied briefly, a frown creasing his brown forehead suddenly.

He seemed to have retreated into himself within the last half hour, Madeleine thought with disappointment. The silence between them was not as comfortable as it had been. He had not spoken at all, and she had been reluctant to penetrate his mood of concentration. Perhaps it was the narrower and more winding road that was responsible.

'There it is!' he exclaimed suddenly, with evident pleasure and pride in his tone, as they curved around a hill.

Madeleine looked and gasped at what she saw. A large white building of rambling architecture was perched amongst lush gardens just this side of a rocky headland. Below was a crescent of white sand against which the lacy foam of waves was rolling gently. Beyond the cove, the sea was very blue, contrasting with the vibrant colours of the garden, whose tumble of grey-brown rocks, dark foliage, pink and purple cascades of flowers and brilliant green grass ran right down to the sand. The hospital building looked cool and quiet with its columned verandahs, balconies on different levels, and big windows, of which many faced the sea.

'It's beautiful,' Madeleine said at last.

'I know.'

Seconds later they were turning into the shaded gravel driveway, and Madeleine did not have time to speak again before the surgeon pulled up in front of what must be the main entrance. A rather plump middle-aged woman dressed in black came out to meet them, greeting the doctor enthusiastically, and kissing Madeleine in the French way—on each cheek—when they were introduced.

'This is Madame Chevet, who is in charge of staff accommodation and catering. She will look after you— ah, Pierre, here you are!' Christian broke off and turned to a cheerful young man who had also approached the car. 'Help me with my luggage, would you?'

He opened the boot, took out one of his suitcases and walked away with it towards the house, without another word to Madeleine. She stood there, unable to listen to Madame Chevet's words of welcome, as she felt the strength drain from her legs, and blood throbbing in her ears.

After the growing intimacy of their journey together, culminating in today's sunny picnic and their lazy kiss, Dr Galantière now seemed to have forgotten all about her.

CHAPTER THREE

'I WILL show you to your room straight away,' Madame Chevet was saying. 'Of course you will want to unpack and settle in. After that, why not come down to my sitting room and have coffee before you meet the rest of the live-in staff over dinner?'

'Yes, that would be lovely,' Madeleine replied mechanically, picking up her suitcase and beginning to follow the housekeeper. She simply did not know what to think of Dr Galantière's sudden departure, and had to force herself very firmly to concentrate on what Madame Chevet was saying.

'It is a small room, but bright and very pleasant, I think you will find.' She spoke in French that Madeleine guessed was deliberately slow and clear for her benefit. 'It is on the east side of the building, so you will get the morning sun for much of the year.'

They had entered through the main door and were now turning and twisting through what was to Madeleine a bewildering series of corridors, steps and hallways. She was sure that she would never find her way about, but then she had felt that way about St Catherine's at first.

'Of course this building was not built as a hospital,' Madame Chevet said now, confirming Madeleine's impression of a rather unusual layout. 'It was a huge private house, but the owners went bankrupt and sold it to some people who wanted to start a school. They made many of the additions and improved the plumbing, but then decided that the building was not suitable after all.

So it became a hospital, with more additions over the years. It is not the most efficient of designs, but everyone who works here comes to love it soon enough, and would not change one brick or window. I am sure you will feel the same.'

'I hope so,' Madeleine replied with a smile.

At that moment they stopped outside a white-painted door near the end of a sunny corridor. Madame Chevet detached a huge set of keys from her waistband and with miraculous rapidity fitted the correct one into the lock.

'I will take this off the ring and give it to you. If ever you lose it, there is a spare one in my office.'

She held open the door for Madeleine, who entered and beheld just what Madame Chevet had described—a white-painted room, modest in size and furnishings but having an atmosphere of light and freshness with its big square-paned window and view of the garden beyond. Beneath the window there was a black iron bedstead with a mattress covered in a white chenille bedspread, and against the opposite wall stood a small white-painted wardrobe and a matching chest of drawers with a swing-glass above it. Next to the bed there was just room for a tiny but solid-looking desk and chair in a dark wood that went with the stained floorboards. Completing the furnishings and adding colour to the room was what looked, to Madeleine's incredulous gaze, like a braided rag rug, large and patterned in gay pinks and blues.

'Is that . . . surely that carpet is very old?' she said in halting French, not being able to think of any better way to ask about the rug on the spur of the moment.

'Old? Why? Do you not like it?' Madame Chevet replied a little huffily, thinking that Madeleine's words were a criticism. She hastened to correct the mistake.

'No, not at all. I love it. But in England these things

are often regarded as quite valuable antiques if they are old and hand-made. I was surprised to see it here.'

'Ah! I understand.' Madame Chevet's face cleared again. 'It *is* quite old. My grandmother made many of them in her youth. I found them last year stored in an attic in her old house and thought they would go well in the rooms here, for a little brightness. I did not realise anyone might want to buy them.'

'You won't take them away now and sell them?'

'Of course not!' Madame Chevet shrugged off the idea expressively. 'They are useful and pretty here. Why should I want to get money for them?'

She left a minute later, after giving a complicated explanation about how to reach her suite of rooms—an explanation which Madeleine did not even understand, let alone expect to remember.

'But I suppose I'll find it somehow,' she said aloud to herself, sitting heavily on the bed and heaving a sigh.

Now that she was alone she could not stop her thoughts from returning instantly to the scene of Dr Galantière's abrupt departure. She felt confused—torn between anger at him and at herself. Had she simply imagined the electricity that had vibrated between them last night and today? Surely not. Had he simply been flirting, then? Frenchmen were notorious for their talent at this pastime, even though Madeleine had wondered in the past if this wasn't more legend than fact.

'If he has been flirting, then I've completely misunderstood,' she realised. 'There could be rules to this sort of thing—rules that he is playing by, and that I don't even know about.'

The more she thought about it, the more likely it seemed that this was the case, and she decided that the best thing to do would be to put the whole thing out of her mind, and into the past. If this decision was wrong, she would soon find out.

Indeed, perhaps even as she unpacked there would be a tap at the door and he would be standing there with some little thing to tell her about the routine at Le Breuil, and a caring enquiry about how she liked her room.

It was dangerous to have thought of this, though, because when the contents of her suitcase were arranged in drawers and wardrobes, and the one piece of decoration she had brought with her—a watercolour landscape painted long ago by her mother—was hanging from a hook on the wall, and Christian had not appeared, she realised that she had been counting on his doing so all along.

Was she wrong to feel angry that he had not made things clearer? She thought back to her feelings about him only yesterday morning and it seemed ridiculous that they could have undergone such a change. Had yesterday morning's feeling been the right one after all?—Oh, the whole thing was stupid! Neither liking Christian Galantière nor disliking him was comfortable, so it would be far better to think about something else.

She left her room and after two or three wrong turns which led to doors into the garden or darkened store-rooms, arrived at Madame Chevet's sitting room, where coffee things were already laid out.

Two young women were sitting with the housekeeper, and Madame Chevet introduced them as Fabienne Noyer and Julie Rondin, two of the nurses at Le Breuil who also lived in. They both had a petite, French style of prettiness, though one was blonde with a round face, while the other had dark hair and high, finely-moulded cheekbones.

'I thought you would like to meet some new faces one at a time instead of all at once tonight in the dining room,' Madame Chevet explained with a matronly smile.

'Yes, it is much easier that way,' Madeleine agreed.

The blonde nurse, Fabienne, laughed and spoke.

'We are very pleased to meet you,' she said in violently-accented English, then lapsed into rapid French, saying something about skipping English classes at school.

'Are you starting tomorrow?' asked Julie.

'I don't know,' Madeleine confessed. 'Madame Chevet . . . ?'

'Dr Galantière did not tell you during the drive?' queried that lady, evidently surprised.

'No, he . . . he didn't.' Madeleine remembered that over lunch on Saturday they had discussed the hospital in general, but not her own role there. She remembered also that it had been the first friendly conversation they had had. 'We seemed to talk mostly about other things.'

'I bet you did,' said Fabienne, laughing again and directing a significant and slightly silly look at Julie.

Madame Chevet frowned as if she disapproved of Fabienne's frivolous comment and began to pour the coffee as she answered Madeleine's question.

'You start tomorrow,' she said. 'I hope that does not seem too soon?'

'Not at all,' Madeleine replied. 'I'd like to settle into a routine. I am on the male surgical ward, is that right?'

'Yes, and it is a very pleasant one too.'

'It is,' Julie put in. '*Oh là, là!* The windows facing the sea! Beautiful!'

'But because you are English we will be sending you to other wards to care for English-speaking patients occasionally,' Madame Chevet explained, then they went on to talk more about the details of hospital routine and the work that Madeleine would be doing.

When the little party broke up twenty minutes later, Madeleine felt that she had put forth the first few tiny roots of friendship at Le Breuil, and was rather looking forward to the evening meal which would take place quite soon.

Madame Chevet had mentioned that about twenty people, members of both the medical and the service staff, lived in the hospital itself. She had not spoken of Christian Galantière specifically, but Madeleine was sure that he did live here and was half-consciously anticipating seeing him at the meal. There, he would surely at least smile and she would understand that they were friends and would spend more time together later.

But the nine tables of diners had finished their soup and were well into their main course of grilled steak and Dr Galantière still had not appeared. Madeleine decided that it was time to stop looking up each time the door opened and closed, and start concentrating on the rapid flow of French conversation around her, trying to understand and if possible contribute.

Fabienne and Julie were both at her table, as well as a young man who turned out to be one of the gardeners and another who was an orderly.

'You came all the way from England with Dr Galantière?' Fabienne asked Madeleine suddenly.

'Yes. The timing was very convenient.'

'And you stayed overnight in a hotel. I'm jealous!' the blonde nurse giggled.

Madeleine felt a faint flush mount to her cheeks. She did not know quite what the other nurse's comment implied, but decided to ignore it. Fabienne continued to speak, however.

'He gave me a lift to Nice once,' she said, 'and then bought me coffee. It was heavenly.'

'You! You are in love with anyone if he is a doctor,' the young gardener said with evident scorn.

'So? It is fun,' Fabienne replied a little petulantly. 'Especially if he is interested in return.'

She giggled again, then turned to Julie and whispered to her in rapid slangy French that Madeleine would have found it impossible to follow, even if the words had been loud enough. She suddenly felt rather dispirited. Fabienne's conversation seemed to add evidence to the idea that Christian Galantière could be charming to any woman if he chose to be.

'Though of course he wouldn't be serious about someone like Fabienne,' she found herself thinking. 'Someone like Fabienne . . .' A young nurse without much sophistication or experience, in other words. Someone like Madeleine herself.

She felt foolish now, and angry with herself because she had not reacted to Christian's casual flirtation as Fabienne seemed to be able to do—admitting with a careless laugh that she found the man attractive but then thinking no more about it, and certainly not entertaining hope of anything serious.

It was depressing, too, that she found the dinnertime conversation so bewildering. Everyone spoke at once, and so fast, and had to make a special effort to slow down if Madeleine was to understand. Would it be like that on the ward tomorrow? She decided that in fact it should be easier. There would have to be a lot that was familiar about the routine, and much of the work of nursing did not involve complicated conversation. In addition, of course, she was tired tonight and unsettled by the newness of her surroundings. After an early night, everything would seem better.

Madeleine's travelling alarm clock woke her at six the next morning. She had slept restlessly as one often does in a strange bed, but the little room was already beginning to seem like a friendly refuge, and she was not depressed as she rose, put on a fluffy cherry-coloured dressing-gown and went along to the nearby bathroom to shower. Breakfast—a simple meal of orange juice, chocolate or coffee and a roll—was at half past six and she was due on the ward at seven.

Friendly Julie, who seemed quieter and steadier than Fabienne, worked on Women's Surgical, which was next door to Madeleine's ward.

'I will take you up there and introduce you to Sister Angèle, who is your senior on this shift. She's a dear. You're lucky. On my ward you would be working under a real dragon—Sister Noelle. Detestable!' Julie grimaced, giving Madeleine's arm an enthusiastic squeeze.

Madeleine fell in love with her new ward at first sight. It contained twenty beds, and although they were not partitioned off into smaller cubicles as most modern wards now were, Madeleine decided that she preferred the airiness of the more open arrangement with its truly glorious view of the sea, the little curved beach, the rocky headland and the gardens, all seen in a panorama from the white-framed windows which ran the length of the ward. Substantial folding screens stood against the walls in the spaces between beds, and these could be used to surround each bed whenever privacy was needed.

Sister Angèle came to meet the two nurses and was very friendly in her welcome, kissing Madeleine as she kissed Julie, once on each cheek. She was a woman of about thirty-five, married with two children and living in Nice, Madeleine later found out.

Julie had to leave immediately to report for work on her own ward, and Madeleine was plunged at once into the routine of work on Hibiscus Ward—or Salle Hibiscus, as it was called in French.

'I won't confuse you with too many long explanations all at once,' Sister Angèle explained sensibly. 'It is better for you to begin work and ask questions as they arise. I'm sure you will find that it is all much more familiar than you had imagined.'

Indeed, this was the case. Sister Angèle took Madeleine on a brief tour of the layout of the ward and its equipment, then put her to work taking observations of each patient's condition and progress. The morning passed quite quickly as Madeleine familiarised herself with the names of her new patients and studied the treatment that each was receiving before or after surgery for their various complaints. She only had to ask for special help from Sister Angèle a few times during the first two hours of duty.

It was at just after nine that Dr Galantière came in to check the progress of his patients, who had been attended by other doctors during his three-week absence.

Madeleine was at that moment about to take some routine observations on a patient at the very end of the ward, who was in the last stages of convalescence after having a dangerously swollen appendix removed. She did not see Dr Galantière at first. The appendectomy patient was a rather good-looking young man—in his late twenties, Madeleine guessed. The name on his chart was Patrice de Brabant, but he laughed teasingly when she said hullo to him, addressing him as 'Monsieur de Brabant'.

'Is my face so creased with pain that I look old to you?' he said. 'Please call me Patrice, as I am sure we cannot be too far apart in years.'

He smiled mischievously at Madeleine, and his green eyes twinkled in his tanned face. She could not resist smiling back, but the smile froze unnaturally as she looked up and saw Dr Galantière at the far end of the ward, listening to Sister Angèle as she talked about the progress of the patient in the first bed.

Had the surgeon seen her yet? Madeleine wondered. Probably not, but of course he did know that she was on this ward. He must be expecting to encounter her. How would he react then? And more importantly, what would her own attitude be? Plunged into the new and yet familiar activities of the ward, Madeleine found that yesterday already seemed distant in the past, and after listening to Fabienne last night, she could not now imagine that there would be anything special in the way Dr Galantière behaved towards her. She made herself concentrate on Patrice de Brabant again, setting up a sphygmomanometer and beginning to take his blood pressure, then his pulse.

'What a pity I am going home the day after tomorrow,' he was saying, still with a crooked teasing smile hovering about his finely-drawn lips. 'I have missed out on two weeks of your tender care. You are not French, I observe. English? Or perhaps American?'

'English,' Madeleine replied, trying not to be distracted as she noted down neat figures on his chart.

She was unaware of the pretty picture she made in the new white uniform she wore, with its smart starched cap. Her eyes cast down over her patient's chart showed off their thick black lashes to full effect, and the calm concentration in her face allowed the delicacy and proportion of its bone-structure to be clearly seen. All this was not lost on Patrice de Brabant.

When Madeleine moved to the last patient and prepared to change his abdominal dressing, she was vaguely aware that the mischievous appendectomy patient was still following her with his gaze. She was more aware, however, that Christian Galantière was gradually moving up the ward, still with Sister Angèle hovering attentively at his elbow. Madeleine concentrated again on her work as the surgeon looked up and seemed to be staring down the ward for a moment.

She saw that she would have to go to the ward store for a new pack of sterile gauze, and realised that her route would take her past Dr Galantière. She made herself walk normally, thinking of the thousands of times at St Catherine's when she must have walked past a doctor without saying hullo, or with just a brief nod and smile. It was impossible to stop herself from hoping, however, that this time there would be some extra little touch of friendship from Dr Galantière—an added warmth in his eyes, or a brief enquiry about how she was settling in.

Sister Angèle seemed to be talking very animatedly, though in an undertone, to him, her hands making shapes in the air and a frown creasing her still-smooth forehead. She and the surgeon were standing at the foot of the bed of a patient who had recently undergone difficult gastric surgery. He had been making good progress in the two days since his operation, Sister Angèle had explained to Madeleine, but during the night he had vomited twice, and his fluid balance chart revealed that there was now a considerable risk of dehydration.

Dr Galantière was nodding at Sister Angèle's words, and, like her, he was frowning—but all the same he was looking directly at the point where Madeleine would be passing in a few seconds. She looked up steadily at him, prepared to smile, but he seemed to look right through her and offered no greeting or sign of recognition whatsoever.

Madeleine did not change her pace or her expression but continued on to the room where supplies were kept and found the pack of dressings she needed, then returned just as steadily to her patient. This time Dr Galantière and Sister Angèle were both bending over Raoul Menier, the abdominal patient, so there was not even the chance that the surgeon would greet her this time.

Madeleine could not help feeling angry and depressed. Christian could not have forgotten that she was due to start on this ward today. Even if their two-day trip together had meant nothing to him at all, it would simply be common courtesy to ask her how she was settling in. Or perhaps he had guessed how strongly she had responded to his attention to her and was trying to communicate to her in no uncertain terms that to him the past two days had not been important.

'Well, I've got the message,' she said to herself as she began to change Monsieur Gatellier's dressing, and when again Patrice de Brabant began to chat to her in his teasing way, she responded in kind and enjoyed their light exchange very much.

A minute or two later, Sister Angèle came down the ward to her.

'Why don't you go along to the nurses' station and have morning coffee, Madeleine?' she suggested. 'I'll have to spend more time with Dr Galantière. After three weeks away, he has a lot to catch up on. But we'll join you later.'

Madeleine nodded and left, unable to stop hoping that over morning tea something would be resolved between herself and Dr Galantière. The coffee and tea-making facilities of this nurses' station were shared between three wards: Madeleine's own, Julie's Women's Surgical, and the men's medical ward where Fabienne worked.

Fabienne was just pouring coffee and Julie had made a pot of tea, rightly guessing that the new English nurse would welcome a cup rather than more of the strong French coffee she had had at breakfast.

Madeleine would have enjoyed the break except that she was waiting tensely for Dr Galantière to appear with Sister Angèle at any moment. Julie made conversation with her, using careful French that Madeleine had no trouble in following. Fabienne was reading an illustrated paper, and seemed absorbed in accounts of the doings of actresses, heiresses, and jet-setters in general. Only once did she look up from her reading to say rather suddenly to Madeleine:

'You're American, aren't you?'

'No. No, I'm not. I'm English,' Madeleine replied, disconcerted by the directness and speculation in the girl's gaze. She stumbled a little over her words, and to her annoyance, felt herself flushing faintly.

'Oh, of course, I see,' said Fabienne, nodding as if satisfied, but still looking at Madeleine with cool interest and assessment in her eyes. 'And your surname? It is Caine, Madame Chevet said . . .'

It was worded as a statement, but the intonation made it into a question.

'No,' Madeleine corrected the other nurse again

patiently. 'I suppose English surnames are a little difficult. My name is Carver. Why? Did you think you had
found a relation of mine in your magazine?'

'Something like that,' Fabienne nodded with a light
laugh. Then she went back to her reading, ending what
had been for Madeleine an awkward conversation.

Julie shrugged, evidently a bit bemused too, and went
back to what she had been saying to Madeleine before
the blonde nurse had interrupted. A moment later Sister
Angèle came in, and Madeleine felt the muscles of her
jaw tighten as she looked for Dr Galantière. But the
Ward Sister was alone.

'Where is Dr Galantière?' Fabienne asked
Madeleine's question for her.

'He couldn't stay,' Sister Angèle answered. 'He is too
busy. That man! He has only been back for a day and
already he is working too hard. One of these days I'm
afraid we will have him as a gastric ulcer patient, and I
am going to tell him so!'

She clicked her tongue and gave a Gallic shrug, then
turned her attention to pouring coffee. Her words had
given Madeleine a new key to the personality of the
surgeon whom she found so disturbing. It seemed he was
a man who cared more about his work than about
anything else. He was not married. Perhaps at thirty-six
he intended to stay that way, and romance had a place in
his life only in the form of light flirtations and occasional
brief affairs.

It was an explanation that fitted everything she knew
about him, Madeleine reflected. Very likely it was the
correct one.

Patrice de Brabant was walking down the corridor
on his way to the bathroom when Madeleine left the
nurses' station to return to the ward with the others.

He wore cream silk pyjamas edged with navy blue piping, beneath a kimono-style dressing-gown in which these colours were reversed, and he looked quite ready to end his convalescence. He grinned wickedly at Madeleine, then dropped two kisses on the cheeks of Fabienne. She laughed and turned around in response to his coaxing that she accompany him a little way down the corridor. Then they chatted together in French that was frankly too fast for Madeleine to follow.

'Fabienne is good fun, and a good nurse,' said Julie in Madeleine's ear, 'but she flirts with any male—patient or doctor—under forty.'

'How does she know Patrice de Brabant? He's not on her ward,' Madeleine said.

'He was here before, about eight months ago, and he was on her ward then—Men's Medical,' Julie explained in an odd tone.

Madeleine did not know what to make of it, but could not ask, of course.

She took a quick look back at the pair as she turned out of the corridor and into the ward. To her surprise they were both looking at her, while Fabienne was still speaking with great animation. Were they talking about her? Perhaps it was natural to suspect so. Madeleine thought that she heard the word 'American', but she must surely have been mistaken. She had already explained to Fabienne that she was *not* American. She frowned as she walked on to the ward. It was annoying to suspect that you were being talked about . . .

Madeleine had no time to think about anything but her work for the rest of the morning, however. Several patients had just returned from surgery, or were due to do so at any time, and the gastric surgery patient,

Monsieur Menier, whom Sister Angèle had been worried about earlier, needed special attention and careful monitoring.

When she came off duty at three, Madeleine had not seen Dr Galantière again, although he had made another brief visit to Hibiscus Ward. It seemed that fate, as well as his own evident wish, was keeping them apart, as she doubted that he had even seen her sitting in the annexe to the ward studying patients' record cards.

The rest of the afternoon stretched ahead emptily. Julie was being picked up by her boy-friend and they were going into Nice for a meal and a film, and Fabienne had evidently arranged something with another nurse. Although Madeleine had met one or two more people over the hot midday meal, she did not feel ready to ask any of them if they were interested in going for coffee somewhere.

She decided to change, then spend some time exploring the nearby village. If there was a café, she would go there and perhaps ask someone about public transport between Nice and Cannes. There were bound to be buses which could take her to some interesting spots on her days off. Antibes was nearby too. It wouldn't matter if she went about alone at first—there was plenty to see and do, and she would soon find good friends among the staff.

As for Dr Christian Galantière—it was getting easier every minute to renew the dislike she had originally felt for him, she told herself firmly, so it certainly wasn't any loss to her that she would not be spending any time with him!

She thoroughly enjoyed her exploration of the village of Le Breuil, which began properly a few hundred metres farther on from the hospital, around a bend in the road which curved up over the rocky headland and looped around another scooped-out bay and hillside. The little town was typical of this part of the country—a higgledy-piggledy collection of houses, mostly made of stone, that clung to and blended with the steep rocky slopes. Riotous tumblings of colourful shrubbery softened the stone and made the whole place seem like something that had actually grown out of the hillside.

Madeleine was content just to wander through the narrow winding streets for nearly an hour and a half, as well as along the seafront where several small boats—fishing vessels or pleasure craft—were moored at jetties. She found several shops, one or two ambitiously modernised, but the others quaint places that might turn out to contain many treasures amongst their oddly-arranged merchandise. On the waterfront there was a little seafood restaurant which she thought she might try one day, and two doors down from it a café.

The place was small and tranquil in atmosphere. Several men who were obviously regular customers stood at the bar chatting to the proprietor and drinking anisette, but Madeleine did not feel awkward sitting at a table by the window with her hot chocolate. The pot-bellied and very cheerful apron-clad owner of the café came up to her as she was drinking it, and the other heads in the café turned her way.

'You have an English accent,' he remarked. 'Are you the new nurse up at the hospital?'

'Yes, I am.'

'Ah! Then welcome to Le Breuil! My daughter works in the kitchen there. I think you have not met her yet, but she has noticed you and told me about you.'

'I didn't realise I was worthy of such attention,' Madeleine laughed.

'Of course you are. Many people in this village work at the hospital, so its goings on are always important news to us,' he assured her.

'How are you liking it?' one of the other customers asked Madeleine after a moment.

'Very much so far, but I've only been here for a day. It's so beautiful with the sea and the gardens, and this village.'

'You will like it more and more, I promise you,' the man replied.

'I'm sure I shall. But tell me,' Madeleine seized on the opportunity to ask about transport, 'I'd like to explore more of the area. Are there buses between here and other towns?'

They told her that there was a regular service which went frequently and was not too expensive, and a few minutes later she left the café to return to the hospital, well pleased with the afternoon.

This was what Father and Jean would have wanted— to see her interested in these new places and people, and already planning to extend her explorations further. It was satisfying to feel, too, that she had thoroughly succeeded in forgetting about Dr Galantière, and all the disturbing and contradictory feelings that seemed to go with him.

CHAPTER FOUR

'Ah! It's my favourite nurse,' Patrice de Brabant said with a grin, after rounding a corner unexpectedly and coming face to face with Madeleine.

She was on her way to the little beach below the hospital on Thursday afternoon after working an early shift.

'What are you doing here, Patrice?' she asked, smiling back at him. 'You were discharged yesterday.'

'I have come to set-tle my ac-count,' he replied, speaking the last words in heavily accented English, then adding carelessly: 'And to see you.'

'To see me?'

'Yes. Are you so surprised?'

Madeleine could not think of a reply, but found strangely that Patrice was right. She was not surprised. He had been openly attentive to her all during Tuesday's work on the ward and she had enjoyed it. His teasing had been so light and amusing, and she had felt that if she had given any sign that it displeased her, he would have stopped. It was nice to feel so certain of his intentions after the disturbing confusion over Dr Galantière.

'I wouldn't be surprised if he asks me out,' she had thought yesterday, when he said goodbye before being discharged, and now it seemed that he was about to do so.

'You're not going to answer my question, are you?' he was saying now.

'Am I surprised?' she said lightly. 'Perhaps not.'

'Then if I ask you to come out with me on Saturday—you see I have already found out it is your day off!—you will accept?'

'Yes, I will,' she said simply.

'Good! Then we will say no more now. I must go and pay my bill before the office closes. I shall pick you up here at ten o'clock on Saturday. You will bring swimming things, and something for the evening, and we will have a wonderful day.' He planted a frivolous kiss on the tip of her nose and walked away.

'Shall I wait in my room?' she called after him, laughing helplessly at the speed with which he had outlined the arrangements and departed.

'Yes. I know where it is, don't worry . . .' He was already gone, amazingly lithe and energetic considering his recent operation.

Madeleine was still laughing to herself as she picked her way down the path that wound through the lush gardens to the sandy curve of beach. Patrice seemed so simple—it was refreshing. She doubted that he meant their outing together to be anything more than a piece of frivolous fun, and decided that that was exactly the kind of thing she was in the mood for. After all, this region was renowned as a place where the pursuit of sheer pleasure was the order of the day. Saturday would be fun.

There were several groups of people on the beach, but no one that Madeleine recognised as being from the hospital. Once, this had been a private beach, and any stranger would have been trespassing, but no one was allowed to own their own beach in France now, which Madeleine thought a very good thing. This cove, although small, was quite big enough to allow her a good stretch of sand to herself, even when there were strangers about.

The water looked inviting—the day was ridiculously warm for late May—but Madeleine decided not to swim today. Quite frankly, she felt too lazy after a long day on the ward, and relished the prospect of simply lying on her fluffy blue towel and tanning the pale skin exposed by her new cherry pink and white floral swimming costume.

The last three days on the ward had been heavy ones—and Madeleine still had not spoken to Christian Galantière. She had been rostered for morning duty each day, and the surgeon had been in theatre then, not arriving to check the progress of his patients until after she had gone off duty in the afternoon.

Sister Angèle seemed happy with the way Madeleine had settled in the day before, and decided that she was already at home enough to start being involved in the more complicated nursing procedures which her training in England had qualified her for.

'You don't seem to be having much trouble with the language,' Sister Angèle had observed.

'No, I'm quite pleasantly surprised,' Madeleine had replied. 'Strangely, it's the conversation and the colloquial language that I find most difficult. Most of the nursing terminology is very similar, as it's based on Latin roots.'

'Yes, of course. I hadn't thought of that,' Sister Angèle nodded.

Nonetheless, coping with a new language added to Madeleine's fatigue at the end of each day, and she decided that it would probably be several more weeks before she felt fully acclimatised to her new working environment.

Preparing for work early this Thursday morning, Madeleine had been certain that she would have to at least say hullo to Dr Galantière today, as no surgery was scheduled so he would probably do his round in the morning as he had on Monday. She had planned her reaction to him in detail: meet his eye steadily, smile and say hullo in a friendly way but with no acknowledgment at all of the closeness she had felt with him—mistakenly!—on the weekend. Answer any questions he might ask exactly as she would answer them if they had been asked by Sister Angèle or Julie. But make it clear if she could that she was quite independent here at Le Breuil, and was unperturbed that the relationship she thought they had begun during the journey together was not, after all, to continue.

Then, incredibly, she had not seen him at all. It was mystifying when a junior surgeon, Alice Sadaume, had come in his place to oversee the progress of his patients, as well as those who were normally under her care. Madeleine wanted to ask about the chief surgeon's whereabouts but, in spite of her earlier planning, was still not sure that she would be able to say his name in a normal way, so she had to wait until Sister Angèle mentioned Dr Galantière herself.

'It's lucky that Dr Galantière was able to look at Monsieur Jancou on Tuesday,' she said. 'If that poor man's complications had arisen today while the doctor is away, they might not have been spotted so quickly.'

'Dr Galantière is away?' Madeleine made herself ask. It was a natural question.

'Yes. You didn't know?'

'No. There are still some things I miss when the conversation is flowing too fast.'

'Of course,' Sister Angèle nodded, then explained,

'He has had to go to Marseille. He will not return until Saturday morning. It is business connected with the administration of the hospital.'

'Really?' Madeleine said. 'I didn't think that a chief surgeon would have very much administrative work to do.'

'No, you're right, but Dr Galantière owns quite a large share in the hospital now, and plans to buy an even larger one in future. He has owned a part of it for several years, but it's only recently that he bought more, and it has given him a lot of extra work.'

'I hadn't realised that,' Madeleine murmured.

'Oh yes. And he is a man who is very willing to take responsibility. He could have left the administrative work to another person, but he prefers to do it himself. I think it is too much for one man, but Dr Galantière has a tremendous capacity for work. I ask myself one thing, though: when does he fit in time for other things which are just as important?'

Sister Angèle had left the nurses' station where they had been drinking coffee, after this comment, shaking her head, frowing and shrugging in a way that was typically French. Madeleine had returned to work too, relieved to hear that there was no chance of seeing the man before Saturday. By then she ought to be feeling completely indifferent to him . . .

Madeleine stayed in her lazy position on the sand, secure in the knowledge that she was well protected by high block-out-factor sunburn cream, until the sun was quite low in the sky, then returned to the hospital building in time to write to Thomas and Barbara Brownrigg before going down for the evening meal.

She sat next to Julie, and they found that each had the day off tomorrow.

'Shall we go to Cannes?' the French nurse suggested, and Madeleine agreed with alacrity.

They spent the time very pleasurably in the jewel-like city that is perhaps most famous for its annual film festival. Julie knew the city well, of course, having lived in nearby Nice for most of her life, but she did not seem to mind Madeleine's tireless explorations and rapturous exclamations over its beachfront promenades and interesting buildings. When they returned home again just in time for dinner, Madeleine felt that the day had begun to cement a friendship between them, and she hoped that Saturday's outing with Patrice would be as pleasant.

Unfortunately it began badly. Madeleine dressed in the bright floral sundress she had worn to her interview with Dr Galantière, and confined her fluffy, rather wayward hair into a high knot at the top of her head. She chose the style to keep her hair out of the way if she and Patrice should bathe, but its effect was to emphasise the slender lines of her neck and the neat shape of her well-moulded head. In a woven straw bag she put swimming costume, towel and other required seaside items, as well as a dress and accessories for the evening.

Patrice called for her promptly and led her out to his car—a sporty silver Jaguar that had Madeleine smiling at its suitability for the lighthearted Patrice.

It was just as they were approaching it that another sports car turned into the driveway. Madeleine recognised Dr Galantière's cream MG at once, of course, and her heart jumped. Christian must have just returned from Marseille. Patrice was parked quite near the main entrance to the hospital building in a spot clearly marked 'Reserved', and the surgeon was forced to stop awkwardly just behind him, no doubt irritated at being denied his special parking spot.

Patrice seemed unperturbed.

'Sorry, Monsieur le Docteur,' he said with a grin. 'We'll be away in a second.'

He put a proprietorial arm around Madeleine and led her to the passenger door of the car, opening it for her and helping her in. These possessive gestures annoyed Madeleine, but she could not protest in front of Dr Galantière. He came up to her open window a moment later and, for the first time since last Sunday's abrupt parting, she found herself looking into the man's too-black and now unreadable eyes.

'I have been wanting to ask you how you were settling in,' he said coolly and carefully.

'Well, why haven't you?' Madeleine wanted to reply. 'Surely there have been at least one or two opportunities?'

She did not say these things, however, contenting herself with a faint smile instead, and a few murmured words:

'Apparently, you've been very busy.'

'Yes, I have. But it seems that you have made yourself at home quite adequately without my help.' He spoke in French. 'I was going to apologise for deserting you, but I see it isn't necessary. With Patrice de Brabant as an escort, you are very well set up—How are you, Patrice?'

'Recovering nicely, thank you.'

'My handiwork did not slow you down for long, I see.'

'Just long enough,' Patrice replied.

'Long enough for what?'

'To allow me to meet Madeleine, of course.'

'Of course,' Dr Galantière smiled coldly, and turned without another word back to his car.

Patrice started the engine of his own vehicle and reversed quickly out of the surgeons' reserved place, twisted the wheel, then roared off down the drive, spinning the wheels and sending up a cloud of gravel dust that must have covered the cream MG with a fine film.

'I do not like that man one bit,' Patrice observed through thin lips as they turned out of the hospital driveway.

'May I ask why not?' said Madeleine. She had been a little disturbed by Patrice's display of aggression, but perhaps he had his reasons.

'Fancy him, do you?' queried Patrice, throwing her a glance. He was still frowning heavily.

'Not at all.' Did she say it just a little too vehemently? 'It's natural to feel curious about such a strong statement as you just made, isn't it? Especially when it concerns someone I work with.'

'I suppose so.' His voice and face had softened now. 'But I'd rather not go into why. I have good reasons. Will you trust me and let me leave it at that?' His smile was lazy and beguiling, and his eyes were clear and confident.

'I suppose I'll have to,' she responded lightly, and tried to dismiss the incident from her mind.

It was difficult to do so. The scene had revealed at least two new things to her. The first was that Patrice had another side to his personality than the boyish one which was all she had seen so far. Still, wasn't everyone like that? The person was rare indeed who could not be roused to anger in certain circumstances, and if his reasons were justified, as he said they were . . .

This led Madeleine's thoughts to Christian Galantière. He had been angry too—cool from the very beginning towards herself, then positively glacial when he spoke to Patrice de Brabant. It was evident that Patrice's dislike was fully reciprocated, and no doubt

Christian Galantière would say that he had his reasons for feeling as he did, just as Patrice had.

It came down to an even choice between the two men, if Madeleine was going to take sides in the matter. Somehow, she felt she had to. If she was going out with Patrice and working with Christian Galantière, she had to feel something about both of them. Half unwillingly she found herself favouring Patrice. She did not know him well, it was true, but so far he had been very straight with her, making it clear that he was attracted to her, and then asking her out in a way that left her ample opportunity to refuse.

Whereas Dr Galantière had flirted with her and encouraged her to respond while he had nothing better to do with his time, and then forgotten all about her, it seemed, until today's perfunctory remark about 'wanting to ask how you were settling in.'

'He's exactly like all good-looking Frenchmen are supposed to be,' Madeleine thought. 'He couldn't resist trying to make me fall for him during our journey, even though he hadn't the remotest intention of doing anything about it if I did. Well, he didn't succeed. He may be charming and good-looking with that gypsy face, but I'm not so easily seduced!'

She turned gratefully and impulsively to Patrice.

'I'm looking forward to today. What are we doing?'

'We're going to Nice. Have you been there before?'

'Never.'

'I'm surprised. You'll love it, though. We'll drive along the Promenade des Anglais, then we'll swim, then I'll show you something of the town. We'll have a late lunch in a beautiful open-air restaurant I know of. Then . . . but wait and see.' He laughed wickedly. 'I'd like to surprise you.'

It all happened exactly as he said, and Madeleine loved it. Even when she thought, as she could not help doing occasionally, of her father and stepmother, it was only to say to herself, 'they would have enjoyed this.' The bustle of Nice was exhilarating, and the passing parade of tourists, jet-setters and ordinary French people endlessly interesting. Madeleine found the Mediterranean warm after the cold seas that wash England's shores, yet nothing could have been more refreshing that the tingle of salt water on her skin. Her hair fell down as she sat towelling herself lazily after the swim, and Patrice put it up for her with expert fingers that held the promise of a caress.

At half past three they were still sitting along with several other lazy diners, in glorious sunshine on the terrace of the restaurant Patrice had mentioned, where they had enjoyed a superb lunch of seafood, salad, rich dessert and wine. Patrice had filled the meal with ridiculously frivolous talk—some of it complete nonsense—and Madeleine had laughed much and enjoyed herself more.

'You look sleepy,' Patrice commented now, after a small silence had fallen between them.

'Not sleepy,' Madeleine replied lazily. 'Just gloriously warm and relaxed.'

'You are a bit pink.'

'And yet I put on block-out cream. It must have washed off in the sea.'

'So much for its claim to be waterproof!'

They laughed.

'Perhaps you are not sleepy, but after four days' work in a new job, I am sure you must be tired. It would be natural,' Patrice insisted. 'I am tired too—I *am* still convalescing, after all. I suggest we go to the house of

some friends of mine. They are expecting us for dinner
and I told them we might arrive early for a lie-down.'

They drove to a large and luxurious-looking house
high on the outskirts of Nice. Madeleine found herself
wondering what kind of people lived here, what they did
for a living, and so forth, and it suddenly occurred to her
that she knew very few of these facts about Patrice's life.

'There's a very obvious question that I haven't even
asked you yet,' she said to him as they pulled up outside
the house. 'What do you do?'

'When I'm not in hospital with appendicitis?' he
teased.

'Yes. I mean, you must work. Are you a . . . lawyer?'
She hazarded the first profession that came into her
head, and he laughed.

'No, I'm in business.' The French word he used was
ambiguous.

'In what way?'

'Finance.' He waved a vague hand. 'Commodities,
securities, I really can't explain.'

'Try—I'm interested,' Madeleine persisted. It was the
truth. She always found it interesting to hear about other
people's work, especially if they did something they
enjoyed.

'I'm afraid you wouldn't understand,' Patrice replied.
'It would take hours to explain, and it really is very, very
dull.'

He gave a lopsided grin and then led the way up a
steep path to the house.

His friends, Tanya and Serge Garcia, were a sophisticated couple, he a banker in his late thirties, and she a
much younger fashion model with exquisite and
obviously expensive taste. Madeleine felt awkward in
her simple sundress, which was by now less than fresh,

and with her hair a little untidy and her face pink and dry.

They had a cool drink, then Patrice explained that Madeleine would like to lie down as well as himself. Tanya raised one delicate eyebrow faintly, and the corner of her mouth lifted too, but she nodded and then led the way to a spare room, of which Madeleine guessed there would be several.

'There you are, Patrice, Madeleine.' She held open the door to reveal a beautifully furnished room. 'There is an en-suite bathroom. Sylvie will call you at six. I hope you'll be comfortable.'

'And which room am I to have?' asked Madeleine, politely but pointedly.

Tanya stared at her for a moment saying nothing, then gave a high laugh.

'Oh, I beg your pardon! I thought . . . Never mind. Come this way.'

Madeleine tried to look at Patrice to see what his reaction to this embarrassing misunderstanding had been, but Tanya stepped between them, then Patrice had closed his door.

'Would you like to be called at six too? The others will be arriving at half past seven.' Tanya had stopped outside another room a few doors farther on.

'Yes, please. Thank you so much for all the trouble you are taking.'

'Not at all.' Tanya smiled beautifully. 'Patrice often stays with us, and we don't mind when he brings a friend.'

She left, and Madeleine explored the room for a minute or two, ignoring the implications of her hostess's last words. This bedroom had an adjoining bathroom as well, already containing huge clean towels and fragrant guest soap. The sheets on the bed were perfectly clean and fresh, too, of course. Madeleine decided that it was a pity to make such a brief use of them and planned to lie down on the quilted satin bedspread instead. Probably it was ludicrous to worry about laundry expenses in a house as luxurious as this, but a thrifty upbringing dies hard, she reflected.

She splashed the salty feel from her face, then hung up the dress she had brought, very thankful that it was the smoky pink cheesecloth, and that she had put in good accessories and make-up. She guessed that no matter how much time she spent dressing for dinner, she would look none too sophisticated compared with the host and hostess and their guests this evening.

The maid woke her promptly at six. In spite of her tiredness, Madeleine had not expected to sleep, and yet in fact she had fallen quite soon into a heavy doze. Now she felt stiff and lethargic, and it was difficult to contemplate getting dressed up for a formal dinner with people she scarcely knew.

A cool shower revived her, however, and she felt able to take a lot of care over her dress. Tonight, amethyst and gold earrings, and a matching necklace, added a sparkle to her face and neck, and she dressed her hair in a soft French roll, leaving a few silky wisps to form a fuzzy halo around her cheeks and forehead. Ironically, the make-up style that the girl in the chemists had shown her three weeks ago in London came in very useful tonight, and Madeleine applied it carefully, feeling pleased with the result.

When she went back into the large *salon* where they had sat earlier, Madeleine found that Patrice was already there, dressed in a dinner suit and laughing lazily as he talked with his host and sipped a long cocktail.

'What will you have, *chérie*?' he asked, eyeing the transformation in her appearance with undisguised appreciation.

Sylvie stood near the door waiting for Madeleine's order.

'Oh . . . um, whatever you have there,' she said awkwardly.

'A Daiquiri? Sylvie, a Daiquiri for Mademoiselle Cai . . . Carver.' He shook his head over the slip in her name, and Madeleine hoped it wasn't the strength of the cocktail which had caused him to make it. She knew nothing about Daiquiris.

Tanya came in a moment later, looking stunning in a shimmering one-shoulder creation of spangled silver. For fifteen minutes they sipped and chatted, then the other five guests arrived all in a bunch, the two men in dinner suits, and the three women in bright, elaborately-finished dresses.

'I'm so furious with Christian for pulling out at the last moment!' Tanya exclaimed.

Madeleine's heart jumped at the name, but that was ridiculous. It was a common enough one in France. She looked at Patrice to see if he had reacted to the name, but he was already deep in conversation with one of the newcomers. Anyway, this Christian *wasn't* coming.

'It means there is no one for you, *ma* Sophie.' Tanya turned to a glamorous redhead who wore a white dress threaded with black bead trimmings.

'What sidetracked him?' Sophie enquired, not showing too much concern.

'Oh, business with someone.'

'Business'—Madeleine assumed this meant financial wheelings and dealings. That certainly didn't sound like Dr Galantière.

'He said he might drop in on the way home if he's not too late, for dessert and coffee,' Tanya was saying.

Introductions were made, then the new arrivals sat down and were served cocktails while Madeleine and Patrice were handed a second glass of their original order. Madeleine had found the first one pleasantly frothy and tangy, but had been unable to guess at its alcohol content. She wished she had been given the chance to refuse a second drink, but now that it had been prepared she would have to drink at least some . . .

It could not be said that Madeleine overly enjoyed the dinner they sat down to a while later. The food was delicious—chilled soup, asparagus soufflé, quail in a rich sauce, and three different vegetables, each dish served with good quality wines—but Madeleine felt out of place in this company.

Her place at the round table was in between that of the oldest of the men, Jean-Yves, and the place set for the unknown Christian. The four men discussed business with a speed and vocabulary that was quite incomprehensible to an English nurse. The women talked of fashion, which was all very well for a while, and then of people, none of whom Madeleine knew anything about. No one discussed films or books, travel or world affairs, or any other subject which might have interested Madeleine enough to help her keep track of the rapid interchanges.

So she sat largely in silence, until Jean-Yves, evidently recollecting his social duties, turned to her suddenly and asked her to tell him all about herself.

'I'm a nurse,' she blurted out, stumbling over the rolled 'r's in the word and unable to think of a way in which to elaborate on the dull statement.

'Actually, she has a very interesting history—you

would be surprised,' Patrice put in with a mysterious intonation. 'Money, intrigue . . .'

'Oh, really?' Jean-Yves paused with a forkful of soufflé halfway to his open mouth and gave Madeleine a surprised look.

She tried not to laugh at Patrice's audacity. It was typical of his flippant but endearing approach to life, she decided. He was evidently trying to smooth her social path for her with this preposterous lie, and did in fact succeed in deflecting attention from her towards himself, for which Madeleine was very grateful. She did not bother to listen to what he said, although she gathered that it was a speech full of *doubles-entendres* that suggested mystery and romance. She flashed him a smile just as he finished the frothy fabrication.

'. . . but she wishes none of this to be known for the present, so I would ask you to respect her little ruse and say nothing.'

Everyone laughed, more wine was poured and the next course was brought in, which turned the subject of conversation to food for a while, from which it naturally reverted to fashion and money again a few minutes later.

Madeleine occupied herself in covertly studying her fellow guests. Each of the women was beautiful in a brittle kind of way which owed a lot to artifice, money and an enormous amount of time. The men—apart from Patrice—seemed older and more worn by time. Jean-Yves in particular had a large paunch and a florid face which, though still attractive in a heavy kind of way, looked unhealthy.

He ate a lot, taking second helpings of each course and not—to Madeleine's critical eyes—chewing his food sufficiently. She also noticed that this was the only glass that was empty every time Sylvie came round with wine.

By the time they reached the cheese course, Madeleine was becoming worried. Jean-Yves had fallen silent now and was frowning. A dew of perspiration glistened on his brow and he had sat back at last, only nibbling on one small piece of Camembert. She was about to ask him if he was feeling all right, but just then the maid came in and announced the arrival of the last guest.

When a tall, black-haired figure entered behind Sylvie, Madeleine's heart fell heavily and her knees went weak. It *was* Christian Galantière, immaculate in a dinner suit whose white shirt was a startling contrast to his heavy tan. She had completely succeeded in convincing herself that her earlier fear was ridiculous, and his presence came as a shock.

He was ushered to the place next to her, and greeted her with a cynical smile.

'Well, this is a surprise!'

Madeleine felt at once and with complete certainty that he had known all along she would be there. Was that the reason he had excused himself from the main part of the meal at the last minute? Or was it flattering herself to think that she was that important to him?

'I thought you said you weren't coming,' Patrice growled from his place almost opposite.

'I finished my discussion with Dr Vignolle sooner than planned,' Christian replied smoothly.

He sat back as dessert was brought in, apparently content not to join the conversation which still revolved around what were, apparently, favoured topics. Madeleine noticed that Jean-Yves was still silent, too, and had pushed away the chocolate and rum gâteau he had been served.

'Having a good time?' the surgeon drawled, leaning closer to her to speak the words in a low tone.

Madeleine was aware of a combination of musk and maleness that was too familiar. She had noticed it exactly a week ago when they had eaten together, and it had been an integral part of the seductive quality of that evening. Then, she had thought that the evening might be the start of something important. Now, hostility and confusion were her strongest feelings in Christian Galantière's presence. She forced herself to answer his question, and her reply was over-bright.

'I'm having a marvellous evening,' she said. 'And today was glorious too.'

'You like these people?'

'Very much—But I could hardly say otherwise, could I? They're your friends.' She laughed on a high note and sipped the champagne that had just been served. Her cheeks felt flushed with sun, but if she had hoped that the drink would cool them, it did not.

'Hmm.' His reply was a noncommittal sound. 'You seem to be fitting in well with them, anyway.' His glance took in her flushed face, then moved away.

Silence feel between them again. Madeleine took refuge in a glance at the other diners. Jean-Yves had pulled his dessert dish towards him and was taking a desultory forkful of gâteau, apparently more from lack of anything better to do than any other motive.

He definitely looked ill. Why didn't he say anything? From politeness, probably, or not wanting to ruin his wife Ariane's evening. He had been red-faced earlier, but was now pale. No one else seemed to have noticed anything. Ariane was speaking to Sophie across Serge, and Christian was staring into the distance at a point in space somewhere above Tanya's golden head.

'Dr Galantière . . .' Madeleine could bear it no longer, her nursing instincts fully aroused. Besides, the silence between them felt so awkward. She leaned towards him and spoke softly, wanting his opinion before she alarmed anyone else. 'I'm worried about Jean-Yves. Look at him. Surely he's ill?'

Christian Galantière turned his head lazily towards the older man and studied him covertly but carefully for a moment, then he leaned across to speak to him, his shoulder brushing Madeleine's own.

'Jean-Yves, did you take your pills before you came tonight?'

'No, I didn't,' the other man smiled faintly. 'Don't tell Ariane—she gets furious! I couldn't find them. But I had been feeling better lately. I thought it wouldn't matter— didn't realise how tempting all this would be.'

He chuckled and waved a hand over the table, then clutched it back to his chest in evident pain. Ariane saw the movement and exclaimed sharply.

'Jean-Yves! You're ill!'

'I thought it would pass.'

'Haven't you learnt yet?' Don't tell me you didn't take your pills!' Her alarm was real.

'I couldn't find them,' he answered, embarrassed now.

'And now all this food! And he was on the phone to New York till all hours last night—some deal had fallen through. He should have got Henri to deal with it.' Ariane addressed Christian first, then the room in general.

'I think we had better put you into Le Breuil for a few days' observation,' Christian told Jean-Yves.

'Is it his heart?' Madeleine asked quickly, in a low tone.

'Yes. He's had a few attacks. Only angina so far, but tonight I would say it is compounded by indigestion, and he won't take care of himself, so we can't take any chances,' Christian replied, also quietly. To Jean-Yves he said: 'We'll go now. No, it doesn't matter about my dessert and coffee.' He waved away Tanya's protest. 'Madeleine, you're not on duty, but would you mind helping me take him down to my car?'

'Of course not,' she replied levelly, ignoring the implication—carried more by the tone than the words he used—that she would resent the interruption of her enjoyment.

They were both on their feet straight away. Christian helped Jean-Yves up and supported him while Madeleine loosened his tie and shirt. Christian's car was parked a little way down the street and Jean-Yves was gasping and out of breath by the time they reached it.

'This fresh air feels good,' he managed to say. The room had been warm, Madeleine realised. Dr Galantière had been right to take the ill man outside straight away.

The front passenger seat was moved back as far as possible to allow Jean-Yves plenty of leg room, and Christian took off the older man's jacket and loosened his belt, giving the car key to Madeleine before he did so.

'There's a pillow and a rug in the boot,' he told her.

'I know.'

She remembered all too well how she had used them herself only the week before, and how he had said then that she looked different when she slept. That must have been the first pleasant thing Christian had said to her.

When Jean-Yves was safely in the car with a pillow behind him and the blanket wrapped around his legs,

Christian got out the black medical bag that he never travelled without.

'I'll give him some anginine,' he said to Madeleine. 'Run back to the house and bring water, will you?'

Quickly she did as he instructed and a few minutes later Jean-Yves seemed much better.

'We'll leave straight away. Tell Ariane that I'll ring her as soon as we arrive and she will be able to come and see him tomorrow.' The surgeon spoke briskly.

Madeleine nodded, trying to meet his gaze as she would if any other doctor was giving instructions to her, but she could not. Christian moved to get into the car.

'Good night, then. I'm sorry I didn't get more of a chance to talk with you.' He spoke lightly, but Madeleine ignored the comment.

'I'm coming back to Le Breuil with you,' she said, 'in case you need help with Jean-Yves on the way.'

'Don't be ridiculous, please,' he said shortly.

'I didn't know it was ridiculous to be concerned for a sick person's welfare.'

'It is when that person's doctor is present and says that there is no danger. He has had this pain before and in exactly the same circumstances. Stay and enjoy your evening.' He gave her a long unreadable look that was very disturbing.

'But . . .'

It was too late. He had already climbed into the car, shut the door, and started the engine. Madeleine watched the car roar away into the night until its red tail-lights disappeared around a corner. Why was it that she would so much have preferred to be in that car going back to Le Breuil than here with the remainder of the evening to enjoy and then the journey in Patrice's silver Jaguar?

Perhaps the question was not so hard to answer. Madeleine had not enjoyed the evening very much so far, and found herself hoping that it would not go on for too much longer. She felt guilty, thinking of Patrice, and how he had seemed so keen that she have a good time. The beach and their lunch together had been wonderful, but it might be difficult to assure him sincerely that she had found his friends good company. Still, with the meal nearly finished now, and the pall cast by Jean-Yves' illness, the party ought to break up fairly soon.

Of course there was tension amongst the little group still gathered around the table when Madeleine returned. Ariane was talking emotionally to Tanya about her husband's previous attacks, Serge and Hubert were discussing exercise programmes and diets that they planned to begin, and Patrice was frowning and sprawling dispiritedly in his chair. Was it anxiety on his part?—or boredom? Madeleine wondered suddenly. She delivered Dr Galantière's message to Ariane, then Tanya spoke up.

'I suggest that we have coffee and liqueurs as we were going to, while we are waiting for Christian's call,' she said. 'Unless you would prefer to go home straight away, Ariane, and ring the hospital yourself from there?'

'No. If Christian is going to call me here, I'll wait,' Ariane decided.

'I suppose the Casino is off, then, is it?' asked Patrice in a neutral tone.

The Casino! Madeleine's heart sank. This must be another part of the surprise evening he had promised her earlier. She ought to look forward to such an unusual experience, but she was already tired and guessed that the excursion would prolong the evening by several hours.

There was an awkward silence while people looked at Ariane after Patrice's question.

'Do you mind if we still go, Ariane?' Tanya queried hesitantly. It was obvious that she wanted to, and Madeleine could see that Patrice did too, but they were both trying to do the right thing.

'Of course you must go,' said Ariane. 'Christian seems to think that Jean-Yves will be fine, so there is no sense in spoiling the evening because of it. I won't come myself, though. I'll go home after Christian's call.'

Everyone looked relieved and the atmosphere became more relaxed again. Coffee and a range of liqueurs was brought in. Madeleine already felt that she had had enough to drink, but Patrice teased her into accepting a glass of Benedictine which she forced down with no pleasure at all. She hated being coaxed into drinking more than she wanted, but Patrice couldn't have known that. He was probably just trying to make her feel at home amongst these people. She would have to find a time to say privately to him later that that wasn't the way to do it.

Christian's call came as people were finishing second cups of coffee. He assured Ariane that her husband was safely settled into his hospital bed for the night, and was being carefully monitored, although there was little chance that the attack was serious.

Ariane left almost immediately, and the rest of the party gathered up fur wraps and dinner jackets, then trooped down to their cars, leaving dirty coffee cups on the table, and Sylvie and the cook still washing up in the kitchen. Madeleine decided that she would feel as though she were living in a hotel if she were Tanya, surrounded by all this luxury and attention.

She felt jaded after the heavy meal and day in the sun, and was very glad that she had managed to sleep before dinner. Patrice obviously thought that seeing the Casino at Monte Carlo would be a great treat for her, and very likely it would be fun.

It would certainly be an experience. The drive along the darkened coastline road was exhilarating, and Madeleine could not take in enough of her first view of the fairytale principality of Monaco. Then all too soon they had arrived at the glittering Casino and were immersed in the opulence of another era.

'We must play roulette, of course,' Tanya insisted, clapping her hands like a child.

The *salons* of this famous building seemed to be quite familiar to her. Madeleine was appalled a few minutes later when Patrice passed over a fat wad of notes.

'Something to play with,' he said with a wink.

'But, Patrice! This is a thousand francs!' She converted the amount to pounds quickly in her head. About a hundred. 'I can't possibly!'

'That is just pocket money,' he laughed, and drew out a much larger wad for his own use.

Madeleine had to admit that she definitely enjoyed playing the game for a while, probably because it seemed more like a movie than like real life in this setting. The Casino at Monte Carlo—subject of songs and stories, and background for more than one spy thriller. She saw Tanya rake in a comfortable pile of chips, then prudently put aside her original stake, leaving only the profit she had made to play on the next number.

'I ought to do this every time I win,' the glamorous model confided. 'But mostly I don't—I end up losing the lot. But tonight I'm determined to go home with at least a franc more than I started with.'

Patrice seemed to be losing his money steadily, but he laughed when Madeleine put the minimum stake on her chosen number—eleven—each time.

'I'm amazed at you, *chérie*,' he remarked. 'I thought you would have more flair, and more *sang-froid*. You are playing like a timid English mouse!'

'Perhaps because I *am* a timid English mouse,' Madeleine retorted.

'Perhaps,' he smiled back enigmatically, then muttered an unconcerned oath as once again his number failed to come up.

Away from the table they drank champagne, which Madeleine was frankly jaded with by now. Water, or a hot chocolate sipped sitting up in bed, would be more to her taste at this hour. They were into the small hours of the morning by this time, and after the rich food and wine of earlier in the evening, Madeleine felt heavy and slightly ill. She was working tomorrow, but fortunately not until the afternoon. Even so, unless Patrice showed signs of leaving soon, Madeleine might find it difficult to get enough rest.

'That's enough for tonight,' Patrice announced about ten minutes later, walking away from the table empty-handed.

'You've lost it all?' Madeleine asked incredulously.

'Yes. Annoying, isn't it?' But he laughed and did not look annoyed. 'I have won before. Anyway, it isn't winning, for me. It's the gesture of throwing the chips down, and the thought of winning dramatically—or of losing. It's a release. But I'm tired now—I'm starting to feel Dr Galantière's nasty scar. Let's go.'

They said goodbye to the others and left. The drive

seemed short because Patrice was still in a lively mood and entertained Madeleine with ridiculous legends about Monte Carlo's past. He *was* fun, there was no doubt about that.

Madeleine had recovered her energy and good spirits by the time they pulled alongside the front entrance of the hospital. Lights still shone in various places where the night staff were on duty, as well as in the foyer and entrance porch, but the place was very quiet.

Patrice turned off the engine and leant across to Madeleine. She knew he was going to kiss her, and indeed the wicked grin he gave openly acknowledged his intentions.

'You're good fun,' she said to him softly.

'Only that?' His arms were around her now, and the words were whispered in her ear.

'How can I tell? So far that's the only side of yourself you've showed me.'

'I'll show you one more side tonight, and we'll leave the rest for later, then.'

'All right.'

His lips travelled across her cheek and found her own. It was an expert kiss, but somehow it didn't arouse Madeleine in the way she guessed Patrice had intended it to do.

'I'm working tomorrow,' she said, moving away a little.

'I know,' he sighed. 'I'll have to let you go, then.'

'It's been a fabulous day, Patrice,' Madeleine said sincerely.

'The first of many?' He asked the question lazily, but it demanded an answer nonetheless, and suddenly she was reluctant to give it. She felt that there was more pressure behind the question than the words suggested.

'Ring me up in a few days,' she laughed, and was noncommittal. 'I'm too tired to think about it now.'

Patrice shrugged and did not press her, but he looked disappointed and annoyed. Madeleine opened the door, but hesitated, feeling that she was leaving him on a sour note. Patrice leaned across to her again and ran a hand through her hair, pulling it down from the French roll in which it had been fastened, then he kissed her again softly. A door shut with a quiet clack in one corner of the big entrance porch.

'I'll ring very soon,' he said.

'I'll look forward to it,' Madeleine replied.

She got out of the car in time to see a familiar dark figure coming along the diamond-patterned tiles. It was Christian Galantière, and as she met his gaze she knew he had seen that last kiss. He looked at her fallen pile of hair and the traces of smudged lipstick at the corners of her lips, gave a faint smile to acknowledge her presence, then descended the steps and disappeared into the night, obviously on his way to the semi-detached apartment he occupied on the opposite side of the driveway.

Madeleine bit her lip, oblivious to the sound of Patrice's car cruising smoothly away. Of course she had every right to go out with whoever she liked, and until as late as she liked, on a day off and when she was not working until the next afternoon, but she sensed disapproval in the chief surgeon's manner. Did he think that his staff should not kiss their boy-friends in the hospital grounds?

Or was he sorry that he hadn't got further with her himself last Sunday noon during his brief flirtation with her? Madeleine felt angry at Christian Galantière for impinging on her tired thoughts, and angry with herself for letting him do so. She sighed, frowned, entered the building, and sighed again. It was definitely time to go to bed.

CHAPTER FIVE

DR GALANTIÈRE was the first person Madeleine encountered on the ward on Monday afternoon. She arrived, punctual as always, at five to three, to find him just about to begin checking the progress of the patients on whom he had operated this morning.

He nodded frostily at her and murmured a greeting that was as brief as it could be. Madeleine accordingly modified her own words and gesture to achieve the same degree of distance, wondering how far apart it was possible for them to get. She was about to pass straight on to the nurses' station to check in with Sister Angèle, but remembered the circumstances of their last meeting.

'How is Jean-Yves' condition?' she asked the surgeon.

'As well as can be expected,' Christian replied tersely. 'He'll go home in a few days, and we can only hope that this has given him enough of a scare to get him back on to his diet and pills.'

He moved away afterwards, and Madeleine could not resist watching him for a moment. He looked immaculate as usual, the white coat he wore during his round open to reveal dark tailored pants and a pale blue shirt against which the tan of his neck was a sharp contrast.

He must barely have slept on Saturday night, Madeleine thought, and apparently he had been busy in his office all day yesterday and on into the night, although he had not visited Hibiscus Ward. This hard work did not show in his face, however, nor in the lithe and alert way his body moved around the paraphernalia of the large ward space. His black eyes were clear, too.

Madeleine herself felt less than at her best. She had had a restless sleep during what remained of Saturday night. A brisk walk along the beach on Sunday afternoon to explore the rocky headland beyond the hospital had not thoroughly cleared her head after the rich food she had had at the Garcias' as she had hoped it would, and the evening shift on the ward had not been easy. Several patients were restless, in their most painful stage of convalescence, and Madeleine had had to forget her own heavy head and aching limbs while she tried to do as much as possible to make the men in her care comfortable and at ease.

Her headache increased as the evening progressed and then prevented her from sleeping for quite some time after she had relaxed into the soothing warmth of her bed in its darkened room. A quiet morning spent on the beach studying her French had done much to restore her, but she still felt seedy and wondered whether she had caught a mild virus. Before coming on to the ward today she had taken two aspirin, and was hoping that work would distract her from her body's state.

Seeing Dr Galantière and feeling his unmistakable coolness towards her had not been a good start to the afternoon.

'Sister Carver!' Jeanne Thierry, the nurse who had worked this morning and was about to go off duty, came up to Madeleine as she stood in the ward annexe reading Sister Angèle's ward reports to catch up with what she had to know about each patient. 'Something terrible has happened,' Jeanne said urgently, in evident agitation. 'I'm so sorry to do this to you just as I'm going off . . .'

'What is it?' Madeleine's heart sank. The normally

calm and responsible junior nurse looked flustered and anxious.

'I've pulled Vincent Hébrard's drip out, just as I was finishing his wash. I have to go or I'll miss my bus. There isn't another one until six going up my way, and my mother's sick.'

She was putting on a light outdoor jacket over her uniform as she spoke, and had hurried off before Madeleine even had a chance to respond. She sighed between her teeth and walked quickly out into the ward. Vincent Hébrard's drip! It was more than a nuisance. Madeleine was tempted to feel very angry with Jeanne for leaving without taking responsibility for her careless action, but she knew that the French nurse had difficult problems at home at the moment.

Anyway, there wasn't time to think of that. Vincent Hébrard was still very ill after his recent operation and the drip would have to be replaced as soon as possible. Dr Galantière was the person to do it, if she could catch him before he left the ward . . .

She looked quickly along the row of white-covered beds. Monsieur Hébrard's still had the screen in place around it after the wash Jeanne had been giving him. Dr Galantière was at the opposite end examining a patient who had returned from the recovery ward a few hours earlier. Madeleine bit her lip. The surgeon would not be pleased about what she had to say.

'May I speak to you for a minute, Dr Galantière?' she said to him. She spoke quietly and clearly, but could not help using nervous hands to smooth the white cotton skirt of her uniform.

Deliberately he took a few seconds longer to finish the last step of his examination.

'It's important,' Madeleine was forced to add.

At that he straightened and turned quickly, his eyes narrowing.

'What is it?'

He was standing quite close to her and it was difficult not to be aware of his height and of the eyes that seemed sometimes like bottomless pools of darkness.

'Vincent Hébrard's drip has come out,' Madeleine said, stumbling a little over the words, but managing to give the information in a way that avoided laying blame on anyone. This was a useless device, however. Christian was already striding down the ward, but he turned and flung a sharp question at her.

'Vincent Hébrard? The bowel resection?'

'Yes.'

'And what do you mean "come out"?' Intravenous drips don't just come out!'

'Well, I don't quite know how it happened. You see, I wasn't . . .' Madeleine began, but the surgeon interrupted her.

'Haven't been getting enough sleep lately, perhaps, Sister?' His query was steely.

Madeleine was furious now herself. He was giving her no chance to explain. Should she press the point and insist on making it clear that it was Sister Thierry who was responsible? No, that was petty. Jeanne had gone home to look after four younger sisters and a mother with influenza. She had enough on her shoulders.

As for Dr Galantière—perhaps if she dared, or if they were friends, she might have suggested that his temper, too, betrayed tiredness, but with their relationship already so strained, that would be foolish and danger-ous. Madeleine ended by making no reply to his ques-tion at all, and he soon spoke again, still tense and quick. They had arrived at the patient's bedside now.

'He's semi-comatose. This is going to be difficult, and I haven't got a lot of time.'

'I'm sorry,' she said quietly.

'It was in his hand before, I see.'

'Yes.'

'Well, I doubt that there will be enough pressure in those veins now to replace it there, but I'll try.'

'Shall I put on a tourniquet?' Madeleine asked.

'Yes, please.' Dr Galantière sighed between his teeth and frowned, intent on the task now as he examined Vincent Hébrard closely. 'We can't lose anything by trying it this way first. Fortunately he is not in a state to be too aware of what is going on.'

'But you think . . . ?'

'I suspect that there is peripheral shutdown. When we do get this drip back into action I want you to increase the flow rate and monitor his fluid balance meticulously—and, Sister Carver, when I use the word "meticulously", I mean it.'

'Of course.' Madeleine could not help speaking coldly.

Naturally, she was aware of what this man's condition required, as was Sister Angèle—and Jeanne as well, for that matter, in spite of her carelessness. Dr Galantière was behaving as though the entire staff was incompetent—with the exception of himself, of course!

Momentarily she thought back to the previous weekend and how narrowly she had escaped falling badly in love with him. Now, she could not be more glad that their friendship had come to nothing! she said to herself defiantly.

Dr Galantière had already inserted the cannula of the drip several times into the old man's limp hand without success. Now he moved further up the arm, looking for a firm vein in the crook of the elbow, but again finding nothing. Madeleine felt helpless simply standing there, helping him only occasionally by adjusting the tourniquet or the position of the patient's arm, but she could not move from his side as he might need her at any time for something more difficult.

She could see that the surgeon was becoming more and more frustrated, though now he was saying nothing to her to vent his feelings. Suddenly the tiredness that she had thought at first he must not be feeling began to show in strained muscles around his face. And wasn't his face drained of blood beneath that dark skin?

But why should I feel sorry for him? Madeleine thought. Getting enough sleep and rest is his own responsibility, and he was willing enough to blame me for seeming tired a few minutes ago!

'Damn this! It's no good,' he said at last, moving away from the patient's bed with a sharp gesture of frustration. 'Get a trolley, will you, with all the necessary things? I'm going to have to do a cutdown to get to a vein, and the sooner the better. He needs the fluid.'

Madeleine hurried off to the nurses' station to prepare a trolley with a syringe of local anaesthetic, scalpel, disinfectant and a number of other items. Simone Pézet, the junior nurse on this shift, was in the office area making notes and checking observations. She looked up as Madeleine went past.

'What's going on?' she asked.

'Monsieur Hébrard's drip got knocked out. Dr Galantière couldn't get another vein, so he's going to do a cutdown.'

'Poor you!' Simone Pézet made a face, then smiled and returned to her work.

Dr Galantière was at a nearby basin, scrubbing up

carefully. The risk of infection was not great, but Vincent Hébrard was old and had few physical resources in his present condition to overcome any complications that arose.

When the trolley was ready, Madeleine helped the doctor tie on a clean gown, then he went to work, dulling the nerves of the barely-conscious patient with local anaesthetic and disinfecting the area. In one precise movement he made a cut along the site of the vein a little over a centimetre long, exposing the subcutaneous tissue, and then at last succeeded in inserting the cannula. It was tied into position, then Madeleine released the tourniquet and attached the needle to the giving set.

Dr Galantière set the rate of flow and sutured the cut.

'Put a dressing on this will you, Sister Carver?' he said, peeling off the transparent plastic gloves he had used.

'And a sling?'

'Yes. A pillow too, I think.'

'Very well.'

'And now, after that completely unnecessary waste of my time, I can get back to the rest of my work.'

His voice was cold and strained, and he passed a hand abstractedly through his wayward hair as he spoke, then massaged a tense muscle in his neck.

'It looks as though I'm not the only one who is tired,' Madeleine ventured mildly, noting this last gesture. She was completely unprepared for the reaction that followed. He had been facing away from her after having removed his gown, but now he wheeled around, clearly furious.

'Do not speak like that to me,' he said, controlled but icy. 'I am responsible for how I regulate my work at this hospital. When there is work that has to be done, I shall do it, and I do not need junior staff members to tell me when they think I need a rest.'

His eyes gleamed darkly and the set of his body was menacing.

'I'm sorry,' Madeleine replied, quelling the start of fear that his anger had caused in her. 'I only wanted to . . .'

'I have wasted enough time on this ward today, thanks to your carelessness,' he interrupted. 'I am not going to waste any more. I have made my point quite clearly. Now please go back to your own work.'

He turned and flung the gown into a linen trolley, then left the ward, and Madeleine could hear his angry rapid strides echoing down the corridor for some time before they were cut off by the distant bang of a door. She was shaken by the scene, never having envisaged such a strong reaction from him. She was still bewildered by it.

If she had had any doubts about the depth of Christian's dislike for her, they had disappeared now, because it could only be dislike that had prompted such unreasonable anger. Madeleine was not used to provoking dislike in another person—especially when only a little more than a week ago, it had seemed to be the opposite emotion he was feeling. For a full minute she stood against the window breathing the fresh sea air that came through the half open frame of glass, trying to become calm enough to forget the scene and continue her work.

Had any of the patients been aware of the drama? Or worse, had Simone Pézet noticed anything? Madeleine looked along the ward and decided that fortunately she had not. Dr Galantière's anger, although intense, had not been expressed loudly. It had been more strongly reflected in his smouldering eyes and the tense set of his body . . .

But there was work to do on the ward. Madeleine took off her cap to brush back a wisp of hair that had escaped its pins, replaced the white arc neatly again, and began to wheel the trolley away from Vincent Hébrard's bed.

By the time she went off to the staff dining room to snatch a quick evening meal, she had managed to squeeze the incident to the back of her mind, if not precisely to forget about it. Of course she had experienced a doctor's anger on the ward before. Theirs was a tense profession, with, literally, life and death responsibility. They could not let any fatigue they might be feeling reflect itself in the quality of patient care, so anger was sometimes their only resource. It kept them alert, and it kept the staff who worked with them alert too.

But somewhere inside her, Madeleine knew that Dr Galantière's anger had affected her differently. It seemed much more personal, more directed purely at her, than the anger of other doctors she had come across. Was this because of Christian Galantière's feelings for her, or because of her own too-complicated feelings about him?

Julie Rondin sat down beside her just as Madeleine was about to begin eating a bowl of thick, steaming soup. They were pleased to see each other, as Julie had been away for the whole weekend after their day in Cannes on Friday.

'How is it going?' was the petite dark nurse's cheerful greeting.

'Not bad,' Madeleine replied, smiling but unable to put more enthusiasm into her tone. Julie picked this up.

'That's not good enough,' she said. 'You like your

work, you're in a new exciting place. I refuse to believe
that you are *blasée* about this gorgeous spot already . . .
And I'm not forgetting that you went out with Patrice de
Brabant on Saturday! I want to hear about it.'

'Curiosity killed the cat. Can I say that in French?'

'Well . . . it sounds a bit funny. What do you mean?'

'It's a saying in English. It means . . . don't ask
personal questions, but I'm only joking,' Madeleine
explained. 'Yes, I went out with Patrice, which was fun,
and I do love this place, but I had a bit of an argument
with Dr Galantière on the ward today.'

It was hard to express her meaning precisely in
French. She wanted to play down the incident, but at the
same time was curious about what Julie's reaction would
be. Perhaps if she recounted a similar experience,
Madeleine would not feel so bad.

'Hm!' Julie made a face and gave a shrug. 'What
about?'

'Jeanne Thierry knocked out an intravenous drip in a
bowel resection patient just before she was due to finish,
and I got the blame.'

'That doesn't sound like Jeanne.'

'Oh, it wasn't her fault. She had to rush off—her
mother is sick. It's just that it took Dr Galantière about
half an hour of fiddling to get it back in. He had to do a
cutdown in the end.'

'Nasty!' Julie agreed. 'And so he was in a temper?'

'Yes. More of a cold rage. Is he often like that?'

It was difficult to ask the question in a casual manner.
Madeleine felt as though she was being particularly
prurient in her interest, and yet it would have been quite
normal for her to discuss doctors at St Catherine's with
one or two of her closest friends amongst the nurses.

'No, strangely enough, he isn't,' Julie said thoughtfully. 'He looks right through you sometimes, when he's had a difficult day, but he doesn't often explode.'

'It must just be me, then,' said Madeleine, trying to speak lightly. 'He's taken a dislike to me.'

'Oh, surely not!' Julie exclaimed, jumping to her new friend's defence instantly.

'Thanks for the confidence in me, but I'm not so sure,' Madeleine told her.

'He's just tired. He's overworked. Forget about it,' advised Julie.

'I'll try,' Madeleine smiled.

'Tell me all about your day with Patrice instead.'

Madeleine launched into an account of the beach at Nice and dinner with Patrice and his friends, playing down the parts she had not enjoyed, and not even mentioning Dr Galantière's presence. But Julie's next words forced her to bring the subject up:

'Dinner at Serge and Tanya Garcia's! Where have I heard those names before? Oh yes, there's a patient being monitored in the cardiac unit who collapsed there that night. Isn't that right?'

'Yes, I forgot to mention that,' Madeleine said lamely.

'But surely if you were there . . . ? Didn't they get you to help?'

'I did help a bit, but Dr Galantière was there too, and . . .'

'Dr Galantière! You *are* being reticent tonight. Was he friendly to you then? Perhaps his anger dates from something that happened that evening?'

'No, he was quite cool then, too,' Madeleine was forced to confess. 'Look, Julie, don't worry about it or try to find reasons. We just don't get on, that's all. I shouldn't have made a big thing about it before.'

'Don't get on! You mean it's mutual? You don't like him?' Julie was incredulous.

'No, I don't,' Madeleine replied after a slight hesitation, wondering if she was speaking the whole truth.

'You must be one of the few people who doesn't, then,' Julie said decisively.

'Really?'

'Heavens, yes. He's so good at his job, works so hard, and is very capable at handling staff and patients. He can be arrogant and distant—sometimes I think it's just that he's so wrapped in thought he doesn't see people—but he's never unfair.'

Madeleine could not quite accept this last thing, but she said nothing.

'Half the nurses have crushes on him,' Julie was continuing. 'Sometimes Fabienne goes for days on end without mooning over anyone else.'

'Fabienne! I thought you said last week that she had her eye on Patrice.' Though Madeleine had not forgotten Fabienne's first mention of the surgeon last Sunday night.

'I said she flirts with him. She flirts with anyone, but she always says that Dr Galantière is the best catch—' Julie broke off suddenly and flushed, staring at the door, then turning quickly away. Madeleine followed her gaze and saw that Christian Galantière himself had just walked in and was on his way to the cafeteria-style service bar to collect a tray and a meal.

She had already noted that the surgeon almost never ate here. In fact, this was the first time she had seen him at a meal.

'Do you think he heard?' Julie whispered anxiously.

'No, I'm sure he didn't. He hasn't taken any notice of us.'

'Still . . . Let's talk about Patrice de Brabant.'

'All right,' Madeleine laughed. 'But what do you want to say?'

'For a start, I hope you're not taking him too seriously.' Julie spoke teasingly, but there was as serious undercurrent to her words.

'Is there a reason why I shouldn't?'

Julie hesitated.

'He's a terrible playboy . . .'

'I've realised that,' said Madeleine. 'I think I can take care of myself.'

'I'm sure you can,' Julie said. She still looked uncomfortable, though, as if weighing up the choice between two courses of action. 'Just make sure you are taking precautions, that's all.'

'Precau . . . Oh! Yes.' Madeleine was embarrassed. It was the second time that someone had assumed that she was already sleeping with Patrice. Was that what he would expect the next time he saw her?

'Look, anyway, I have to go,' Julie said quickly after glancing at her watch. 'Florence will be wanting to come off for her meal. Let's go out for coffee some time soon, shall we?'

'Yes, I'd like that,' Madeleine nodded. It sounded as though Julie might have a few interesting things to say on the subject of various personalities at Le Breuil, as well as being a very pleasant companion.

Madeleine finished her own meal in a few minutes, willing herself not to look over to a distant corner table where Dr Galantière ate quickly while talking to Dr Dumant. Had he noticed her? She had not caught him looking her way, but that meant nothing. Probably he had seen her, then dismissed her from his thoughts again immediately. After all, the little that they had to say to each other could be said quite easily when they met on the ward.

For several days after this they did not meet on the ward. Madeleine was transferred to the paediatric unit where there were two American children, one aged six and one nine-year-old, who spoke to French at all. The younger had a severe ear infection and the other child had broken her leg badly during a fall from a horse and was in traction. Both responded so well to her care and the familiarity of her language in a world where everything else seemed strange and frightening that Madeleine overstayed her normal shift by two or three hours each day to read to them or give them other special care.

It was on Friday afternoon that she received a summons to Dr Galantière's office on the ground floor of the central building.

'You are to go when you come off duty at four,' the Sister told her, having taken the message by internal telephone from the doctor's secretary.

Madeleine had no idea why he would want to see her. A new instruction about her hours and the ward on which she was to work next week? No, that information could easily have been delivered by Madame Chevet, Sister Angèle, or several other people. News from Thomas and Barbara Brownrigg? It seemed unlikely. They would write to her personally. Something she had done wrong? That was too awful to contemplate. Anyway, she had made no mistakes that she knew of.

Madeleine ran through the possibilities as she walked down there after coming off duty, wishing that she did not have this cloud on an otherwise clean horizon. The system of corridors and stairs was becoming familiar to her now as Madame Chevet had said they would, and there was an enormous satisfaction in walking through this pleasant building, with its frequently-glimpsed views of the sea.

The afternoon was sunny, as most afternoons had been in the twelve days since her arrival. Twelve days! It seemed longer than that. Ten of the days had been spent at the hospital, but Madeleine was due for three days off, starting this Sunday. She was looking forward to getting out somewhere, although as yet she had no definite plans for the time, not knowing whether to count on Patrice ringing to ask her out.

Did she want him to? That was something else she could not decide to her satisfaction. Sometimes, when she thought of the fun-filled day they had had together last week, she definitely did want to see him again. But then Julie's cryptic warning that perhaps he was less straightforward than he seemed came back to Madeleine. What had she meant? And why had she not said straight out what was in her mind?

This was where language became a problem. Madeleine's French improved every day, and she was beginning to realise that she had a well-developed ear for languages, but there were times when she felt lost. There could be nuances in what someone was saying to her that she was missing completely . . .

Madeleine turned into the last corridor and brought her thoughts back to the interview ahead. Instinctively she smoothed the skirt of her simply-cut white uniform and adjusted the arc of the cap on her black hair that was neatly folded into a French roll on the back of her head.

Dr Galantière's secretary, a thin fair woman in her mid-fifties, looked up when Madeleine entered.

'Dr Galantière asked me to come and see him at four,' she murmured.

'Really?' Madame Courault seemed surprised. She pulled a small memo pad towards her. 'Oh yes, there is a note here. He has changed his mind.'

'Changed his mind?' Madeleine echoed stupidly. 'You mean he's not here?'

'That's right. Do you want to leave a message for him?'

'No. It's only that . . . You don't know what he wanted to see me about?'

'I'm afraid not. But I'm sure he will catch up with you another time.'

'Yes, I daresay he will. Thank you. Goodbye.'

Madeleine left the office again, bemused and unsettled. She did not know what to think now, and was afraid that she would go on apprehensively wondering about the surgeon's appointment with her and its cancellation until he contacted her again. Which would be goodness knew when.

'Sister Carver!' The operator at the main switchboard called to attract her attention as she passed through the foyer. 'How fortunate that you should be passing—there is a call for you. I'll connect it at the wall phone by the magazine table, shall I?'

'Yes, thank you,' said Madeleine, thinking that it could only be Dr Galantière, perhaps to apologise for not being there to see her.

'Hullo, my darling!' A voice spoke caressingly in French at the other end of a crackling line.

'Doc . . . oh, Patrice!' To her relief, Madeleine had recognised him just before blurting out Christian Galantière's name.

'You sound surprised,' he commented.

'A bit.'

'And yet I said I would ring.' He seemed hurt, but perhaps he was simply teasing.

'It's only that I've just come off duty,' Madeleine explained. 'I'm still in my uniform, and I'm still thinking about nursing.'

'You take your work far too seriously, my love,' Patrice chided lightly. 'There is no need to put on such a virtuoso performance. I'd better take you out and give you some fun.'

'Is that a definite offer?' she asked.

'Of course. What about some boating?' he suggested.

'It sounds good.'

'It will be.' He did not comment on the slight pause that had come before her reply. 'Shall I pick you up at nine? Is that too early?'

'Not at all,' she assured him. 'There's just one thing . . .'

'What is that?'

'You haven't told me what day.'

'But tomorrow, of course.' He seemed surprised.

'Oh, Patrice, I can't! I'm working.'

There was a pause at the other end of the line.

'That's a pity,' he said. 'But couldn't you arrange a swap with someone?'

'I don't think so, not at this late stage. All the nurses with days off will have made plans already,' she said with real regret.

'Come anyway. Just take the day off,' he coaxed.

'That would be impossible!'

'Why? I do it,' he said unconcernedly.

'But you're in a completely different kind of occupation. In a hospital—for me, anyway—it's out of the question.'

'Yes, I suppose when you live in, it's not easy,' Patrice agreed, completely misunderstanding her meaning. 'Still, how long are you planning to lie low at Le Breuil? Perhaps it doesn't matter if they think you're a little unreliable when you're only going to be here a few weeks.'

'I don't understand you, Patrice,' Madeleine said patiently and a little coldly. He seemed to be assuming that she had no sense of professional responsibility at all. Then suddenly he seemed to cheer up again at the other end of the line.

'Sorry I sounded cross,' he said, his voice cajoling and caressing. 'I'm like a child in that way—I can't bear to be disappointed. But I get over it soon enough. Now I have to go—I have an appointment. But I'll see you soon.'

'Yes. Goodbye, Patrice,' Madeleine smiled into the phone, then replaced the receiver, having forgiven him.

She felt quite safe in enjoying Patrice's conversation and company. He was a complete flirt, Julie was right, but her worry had been unnecessary. Madeleine was perfectly in control when it came to Patrice de Brabant. It was Christian Galantière who had her more confused at the moment.

CHAPTER SIX

HE stood outside her door later that evening when she answered the knock. He was dressed casually in grey wool pants, a matching V-necked jumper and a white shirt that was open at the neck. Madeleine herself wore a cotton nightdress covered by her cherry-pink chenille dressing gown, which she pulled more closely about her when she saw who it was.

She had expected it to be Julie or another one of the nurses. It was only just after eight, but Madeleine had decided to spend the evening quietly in her room writing postcards to the Brownriggs and several other friends. Now she stood there stupidly, not knowing whether to invite Dr Galantière in to take a seat on the one chair in the room, or leave him standing in the doorway.

'I'm sorry, you were already in bed,' Christian said levelly.

'No, I wasn't,' she assured him. 'Come in . . . if you like. I was just writing a postcard to Thomas and Barbara.'

She waved the coloured card vaguely in one hand, having made the remark simply to cover an awkward moment, but Dr Galantière picked up on it.

'Oh, really? Have you heard from them at all?'

'I had one letter four days ago. It had crossed with my first one to them in the post.'

'Then you are obviously good friends. I hadn't realised.'

'Oh yes,' said Madeleine, still speaking just for the

sake of it. 'They've been so good since . . .' She paused.
Christian Galantière knew nothing about her parents, of
course, but she had gone too far to stop now.

'Since?'

'Since my father and stepmother died seven months
ago.'

There was a small silence during which he looked at
her with an unreadable expression, then he spoke
slowly.

'I didn't know. I'm sorry.'

'How could you have known?'

She turned away, suddenly unable to look at him. And
why on earth was he here? It felt very strange. She
thought of the time at their hotel in Fontainebleau when
he had seen her in her nightdress, sitting up in bed after
breakfast. She hadn't minded that at all because of how
things were between them then, but this was different.

'I wish I could offer you coffee . . .' she said
desperately.

'It doesn't matter. I'll only stay a minute.'

He glanced down at her dressing gown and she was
embarrassed by its dowdiness, not realising how the
bright colour enhanced the new glow in her cheeks and
contrasted prettily with her blue eyes and dark hair, nor
how the simple girdle knotted at her waist emphasised a
neatly curved figure very adequately.

She turned to the chair at the desk and moved it
towards him, then sat down on the bed, very upright. It
was far too awkward for them both to keep standing.
Christian sat down with a murmured thanks, then spoke.

'You'll think this strange, perhaps,' he said. 'I called
you down to my office to say it, but it did not seem
appropriate there. I've come to apologise . . .'

'Apologise?'

'About my anger the other day. Sister Thierry explained later that it was she who had knocked out the drip. I didn't give you time to tell me that, and then what with the whole infernal procedure of getting it back in . . .'

'It doesn't matter,' she interrupted. An apology was the last thing she had expected from this man who was normally so cold towards her now. 'I hadn't thought any more about it.'

This was far from the truth, but never mind.

'Hadn't you? Then perhaps I need not have said anything,' he said in a neutral tone. 'However, there was another reason for my visit. I have had a letter from Dr and Mrs Brownrigg too.'

'Oh, really? Is there some news?' Madeleine was eager at the same time apprehensive. There must be something unusual in the letter if he had specially come to her room to tell her. She hoped it was good news.

'Not news exactly. Thomas has had a letter from your brother. His company have sent him to Marseille on business for ten days. He will be there until Wednesday of next week, apparently. Thomas knows that I have a sister in Marseille, whom I visit fairly often, and he has asked me if I could take you in to see your brother next time I am visiting Irène. I have decided to go on Sunday. You have that day off. Will you come?'

'Yes, of course. It will be wonderful to see Richard. If you're sure that . . .'

'Will you be at my car by nine, then? You know where it is parked.'

'Yes, very well.' She was taken aback by the speed with which the day was being arranged. 'Is there anything I should bring?'

'Nothing special.' He rose to his feet. 'That's settled, then?'

'Yes.' What else did they have to say to each other, after all? 'Thank you for this.'

'Not at all.'

He left after a brief goodbye. He had only spent five minutes in Madeleine's room, but his presence had unsettled her for the rest of the evening. She was pleased to think of seeing Richard. He could not often get to England, and it had been months now since he had even rung her. Dr Galantière was thoughtful to realise that she would want to spend time with him, she had to admit that.

—But no, of course not. It had not been his idea at all. Dr Brownrigg had written a letter to make the suggestion, and it was out of friendship for the English doctor that Christian had complied with it. His apology, too, had not been made freely, but had been a necessary preliminary to the invitation.

For a minute Madeleine toyed with the idea of cancelling the day, but that would mean missing out on seeing Richard, and who knew when his busy life would bring them near each other again?

Madeleine sighed. She would have to bear Christian's company for the sake of Richard. It would be as the first part of their last drive together had been—full of cold, awkward silences.

As for that second day, the day when they had conversed easily, and when there had seemed to be more than warmth between them, as well as the kiss she still could not think of without heat coursing through her veins—it all seemed like a dream to Madeleine now, part of another life. The Christian she had thought she was getting to know that day bore no relation at all to the man she now knew.

'What will I do if he tries to flirt with me again on Sunday?' she found herself thinking. 'I'll freeze him out utterly, of course. But it was ridiculous even to contemplate the possibility. Whatever superficial temptations he might have felt two weeks ago, they were thoroughly drowned out now by a deeper dislike that was quite mutual.

It was Patrice's car that Madeleine encountered first when she arrived outside the main entrance of the hospital at just before nine on Sunday morning, wearing a canary yellow sundress sprinkled with small white dots and with matching white bands at neck, arms and hem.

Dr Galantière's car was in its usual place, but there was no sign of the French surgeon. Patrice de Brabant jumped gaily out of his sporty vehicle and planted several kisses on each side of Madeleine's mouth—the last one resting against the corner of her lips much longer than it should have done. He was wearing expensive-looking white canvas pants, a matching jacket, and a sailor-striped T-shirt.

'Patrice! What are you doing here?' Madeleine exclaimed, admiring the sun and breeze playing on his fair hair. It was good to see him unexpectedly like this.

'It's my consolation prize—and yours too, I hope—for not being able to see you yesterday,' he replied wickedly. 'I thought I would just turn up on the spur of the moment and whisk you off somewhere . . . Why, what's the matter?'

He had seen her face fall.

'I can't come, Patrice. I'm going to Marseille with Dr Galantière.'

'With Dr Galantière? So that's the way things are developing now!' His green eyes had grown cold, so she hastened to reassure him.

'No, it's not that. My brother is there on business for a few days. I'd like to see him, and Dr Galantière is giving me a lift, that's all.'

'I can take you,' Patrice said. 'We'll have a great day. Wouldn't you rather go with me than with him?'

He smiled beguilingly and put his arms firmly around her. Madeleine did not know how to reply. She was quite sure that Patrice would be a better companion than Christian, now that her relationship with the surgeon was so strained, but the arrangement had already been made. She could not back out of it now.

Christian came out of the main building at that moment, descending the steps at an animated pace in his dark pants, pale blue shirt and grey jacket. He stopped and frowned when he saw Patrice, who was still holding Madeleine closely. He offered a terse greeting, which Patrice responded to in kind, then addressed Madeleine.

'Are you ready?'

'She's coming with me,' Patrice cut in.

'I think not,' said Christian.

'I've offered to take her into Marseille, to save you the trouble. You should be grateful.' Patrice's smile was insincere.

'But as I am going into Marseille in any case, it would not be saving me trouble,' Christian countered smoothly.

'Madeleine?' Patrice appealed to her.

'Dr Galantière and I did already have this arrangement,' she said slowly.

Patrice shrugged and released her.

'I'll see you some other time, then . . .' He climbed

into his car and roared away, leaving an awkward silence between the surgeon and Madeleine.

'I'm sorry to have spoiled your day,' said Christian in a neutral tone.

'You haven't,' she assured him.

'And yet naturally you would have preferred to be with Patrice. Unfortunately, however, he does not know which hotel your brother is staying in, nor what time he is expecting you, and I do. Shall we go?'

They were well on their way before any further words had passed between them, their positions in the car and the mood that lay over them inevitably reminding Madeleine of the first day of their journey to Le Breuil together.

'It's a glorious day,' she said, desperate to break the silence and speaking with false brightness.

'Yes . . . And I suppose you are looking forward to seeing your brother?'

'I am. It's been months since I've seen him.'

There was a little pause.

'He did not return to England when your parents died?' Christian's tone was softer now.

'Only for a week. He couldn't get any more leave than that,' Madeleine replied briefly.

'Then a lot of the responsibility must have fallen on your shoulders?'

'It did. It was very difficult. I'm only just beginning to be able to feel normal again.' She gave a brittle laugh and wound down the window of the car to feel the fresh tang of the sea breeze on her face.

'I'm sorry. We won't talk about it.'

'It's all right. But . . . tell me more about your family,' Madeleine said desperately.

It was too unsettling to be travelling with him again

like this, although considering that awkward brush with Patrice, the surgeon was being quite pleasant. Probably, like Madeleine herself, he had decided that antagonism was pointless, since they were forced to be together.

Madeleine was reminded too strongly of the way it had been two weeks ago. But she must not be! What if he began to flirt with her once more? If he tried to kiss her again, and again she responded when she knew now that such things meant nothing to him, she could know no pride.

Why are my feelings so confused? she wondered angrily.

'My family . . .' Dr Galantière was saying now. 'What do you want to know?'

'Oh . . . well . . . Brothers and sisters, I suppose. What your parents do. I didn't mean to sound inquisitive.' With difficulty she brought her thoughts back to the question she had asked him.

'You're not. Let's see, then. I have no brothers, but three younger sisters,' he said, not coldly. 'My mother died when I was fifteen and the youngest was two. My father was—and still is—a very busy man, so I spent the next three years trying to take our mother's place.'

'That's an unusual experience for a boy,' Madeleine remarked.

'Perhaps. I certainly learnt a lot from it, and it was during that time that I realised I wanted to become a doctor. I went to Paris. We were living in Algiers, as we had been all my life until that point, so it was quite a change.'

'Algiers? I hadn't realised.'

'Yes. I'm a creature from even warmer climes than this, though my father was originally from Paris, and lives there again now with my youngest sister Marie.'

'So the one you are going to visit today is . . . ?'

'Irène, the eldest. The middle one, Anike, is still in Algiers. She is married there and is a welfare worker.'

'You wouldn't get to see much of her,' Madeleine remarked.

'No, unfortunately. My work keeps me much too busy. I don't even get to Paris very often.' He laughed ruefully and took a hand off the wheel to pass it through his thick black curls. 'I hope to manage a week's holiday in Algiers this year. I hanker after the place sometimes.'

Silence fell after this. The surgeon's thoughts seemed to have returned to some complex subject, no doubt related to his work, as he was frowning each time Madeleine ventured to glance at him. She felt less awkward after their conversation. It had established a truce between them if nothing more.

Now the scenery commanded her attention. They were following the coastal route, and magnificent vistas abounded. By noon they were driving through the outskirts of the city, and nearly three hours had passed without Madeleine having tired of the sights she saw.

Dr Galantière drove straight to the centrally-located hotel where Richard Carver was staying.

'You'll have lunch and spend the afternoon with your brother,' the surgeon said. 'Will it be convenient if I pick you up at four?'

'Yes, if that fits in best with your own arrangements. You won't come in and meet my brother?' Madeleine felt that this was an invitation he would safely refuse, and she was right.

'I can't, I'm afraid. I have too much else to see to.'

'You're not going straight to your sister's?'

'Later.'

Madeleine got out of the car and he drove off, leaving

her with a strange sense of disappointment. It was disconcerting to find that in spite of everything she could not feel as hostile to him as she wanted to. Sometimes it was possible, but then he would turn round and begin being more pleasant to her, as he had this morning. No wonder she was confused!

Madeleine gathered her thoughts and stopped looking along the street down which the surgeon's streamlined car had disappeared. It was time to go in and meet Richard. She hurried up the steps and went into the hotel.

He was waiting for her in the foyer, a tall lean figure as he stood leafing through a magazine. It was very good to see him again. They clung to each other for several seconds, then he led her into the hotel restaurant where they enjoyed a delicious lunch of salad and chicken on its umbrella-shaded terrace.

Madeleine had always loved Richard with an intensity that in her childhood had bordered on hero-worship. He was seven years older than her and had always enjoyed taking a lead in childhood games, bossing her around, if the truth were told, whenever he thought he could get away with it. Now, of course, their relationship had matured, but they were still as close as a brother and sister could be when they were so separated by geographical distance.

Madeleine enjoyed her long walk with him through the streets of the old part of the city, as they exchanged news about their lives and work, and about Richard's wife Beth and their two small sons. Later, they stopped for a cool drink, and it was with regret that Madeleine told him they would have to start back to the hotel soon if she was to be there when Dr Galantière called for her at four.

'Yes, we mustn't be late,' Richard agreed. 'It's nice of him to have brought you all this way. I spoke to him on the phone to arrange the details—he rang me when he got Thomas and Barbara's letter saying I would be here, as of course you know—and I thought later that I should have suggested that I hire a car and drive up to Le Breuil to see you there.'

'I've enjoyed the trip, though,' Madeleine said, wondering if she were speaking the truth. 'Some parts of the route are fabulous. Anyway, Dr Galantière has a sister here that he wanted to see.'

'Still, I'm grateful to him for our afternoon,' said Richard. 'What's he like?'

'You'll meet him when he comes to collect me, I expect,' Madeleine said evasively, but Richard was not satisfied.

'Good to work with, though?' he probed. 'And looking after you properly here in France?'

'Oh, Richard! It's not his responsibility to do that!'

'Isn't it?'

'No! He's in a very senior position, and I'm only a junior Sister. I'm expected to look after myself, and I can and do.'

'But you drove all the way from England with him—a two-day trip,' Richard persisted—unusually, for him. 'Surely you must have begun a friendship in that time, unless you can't stand the man.'

'Hmm . . .'

'Madeleine, I want an answer!'

'Well . . . Yes, I suppose I like him.' Was it the truth? 'He was friendly and did "look after me", as you put it, on the trip. Now I'm finding my own friends among the nurses, and he's very busy with his work. We don't see much of each other. But why is this important?'

Richard sighed.

'I was going to save this news until it's definite, but I can see I'll have to tell you. There's a strong chance that I'll be sent to South America for two years.'

'Oh, Richard!' she gasped.

'I'm looking forward to it, and actually it will be much better for Beth and the children than where we are now. But it seems even farther away from you—although I suppose with air travel it isn't really. So I'm anxious to know that you have enough support here, if you're going to stay, someone you can turn to. Is Dr Galantière married?'

From Richard this was a most unusual question.

'Richard, you're not trying to find a husband for me!' Madeleine exclaimed.

'Are you so opposed to the idea of marriage?'

'No, of course not, but I'll think about it when I meet someone who . . . who . . .'

'Then I take it that Dr Galantière couldn't be that someone?' He flung her a searching look that made her blush unwillingly.

'Good heavens, no! It's out of the question!' Why did she find the idea impossible to look at too closely?

'Very well, I'll say no more about it,' Richard conceded at last. 'Sorry if I pestered, but I don't want to think that you'll feel very alone when I go off to South America.'

'Just knowing you are concerned makes me feel I'm not alone,' Madeleine assured him, and gave his arm a sisterly squeeze as they arrived once again at the white-columned entrance of the hotel.

They were a few minutes late and Dr Galantière was already waiting in the foyer. He stood up as they approached, greeted Richard and shook his hand heartily. Madeleine was surprised at the warmth of their meeting.

'You act as if you already know each other,' she said, looking from one to the other with a perplexed smile.

'We had quite a long chat on the phone,' Richard explained, then turned to the surgeon. 'What are your plans? Can you stay for coffee with me?'

'I'm afraid not,' said Christian. 'I've already arranged for us to have an early meal with my sister.'

Madeleine was surprised.

'I thought you were seeing her this afternoon.'

'No, perhaps I didn't explain. I had people to see in connection with work. Irène lives on the outskirts of the city, just off our homeward route, so it was more practical to see her on the way back to Le Breuil. I hope you don't mind.'

'Not at all.' It wasn't quite the truth. Madeleine could not imagine feeling anything but awkward during a family meal with Christian Galantière! But she could not say that, naturally.

She and Richard had their farewell—almost a tearful one on Madeleine's part as she did not know when she would see him again, although he had promised to write. Then she and Dr Galantière were again beside each other in the car.

His sister Irène lived in a modest-sized apartment in a rather ugly sprawling block, but Christian explained that she and her husband were in the process of buying a bigger and more attractive place in preparation for the birth of their third child, which was due any day now.

Irène, who met them at the door with a welcoming smile, was a smaller, darker and plumper version of her brother—though Madeleine thought that she probably had none of the on-again-off-again charm and coldness that Christian seemed to exhibit. Madeleine was not made to feel awkward at all as she was drawn into the circle of the family gathered in the crowded living-room.

Irène's husband, Yannick, a chemical engineer, was as smiling as his wife as he served cool drinks, and the two children—a boy of six and a three-year-old girl— were endearingly rough-and-tumble characters who climbed unceremoniously over their uncle in a way that Madeleine would not have imagined possible.

After general conversation and games with the children had taken up a pleasant hour, Irène served a simple meal of eggs, buttered noodles, cheese and tossed salad. She and Yannick apologised to Madeleine, saying that anything more elaborate was beyond them now until after the new baby's arrival, but Madeleine thoroughly enjoyed the plain fare and family atmosphere.

She tried not to look too often at Christian. It was too disconcerting to see him like this—the startling white smile in his tanned face coming very frequently in response to the children's questions and comments. It was odd, too, to hear him addressed as 'Tonton', the baby word for Uncle in French.

'What's the most French thing there is, Tonton Christo?' little Laurent asked. 'Our teacher wants us to find out. I think it's cheese, but Maman says they have cheese in lots of countries.'

'She's right, but let's see. The most French thing . . .' Christian mused. 'What strange ideas your teacher has. What about the Eiffel Tower?'

'What's that?'

'It's a famous building in Paris. One day I'll show you a picture of it, although I'm sure you must have seen one before without knowing what it was called.'

'I haven't! I haven't' Marie-Laurie exclaimed, jumping up and down.

'Then you shall see one too,' Christian promised, chucking her under the chin and picking up her forgotten spoon to coax in another mouthful of egg.

Madeleine could not help laughing delightedly, but when Christian caught her gaze with his own dark eyes, she turned away, embarrassed again, then only a minute later found herself thinking: 'What a lovely father he would make!' as Marie-Laurie came up with yet another impossible and adorable three-year-old's question.

Madeleine caught Irène's eye on her more than once, too. The older woman's gaze was speculative in a way that once again made Madeleine hot and a little embarrassed.

'She's guessed that I'm attracted to Christian,' Madeleine realised. 'But she can't know that I don't want to be, and that he dislikes me so much.'

She looked down at her place for a moment to cover her confusion, then turned to little Marie-Laure and joined in the discussion about 'the most French thing there is' which was still going on.

'Is ice-cream a French thing?' Marie-Laure asked, and Yannick laughed.

'No, my little *gourmande*, but you shall have some for dessert anyway.'

He started to get up from the table as everyone had finished their main meal, but Irène stopped him.

'I'll go. I feel like a little stretch.'

'All right, *chérie*.' He leaned across to give her a supportive squeeze, then turned to Christian. 'So how is the hospital?'

Madeleine watched Irène pull herself to her feet and wince as she rubbed her lower back. In a few minutes she had returned with ice-cream for the two children and a bowl of fruit for the adults. Again Madeleine noticed the worried wince that crossed Irène's features and the careful massaging of her back just before she sat down. Her baby was obviously going to make an appearance within the next day or two.

Christian and Yannick were still absorbed in talk about the hospital, which now caught Madeleine's attention.

'How is the welfare programme going?' Yannick was asking.

'Better even than I had hoped,' Christian replied with sudden animation. 'I'm beginning to convince people that the idea can work, that we can take in a few hardship cases which the government hospital system or welfare agencies have come across, and treat them in our hospital without disrupting routine or creating tension. You remember the little boy I told you about who had been taken from his parents after prolonged cruelty?'

'Yes. That was an awful case,' said Yannick. 'And apparently he lived quite near here.'

'Yes, that's the one,' Christian nodded. 'One of our private patients wants to adopt him. We're starting the formalities going on Monday.'

'That's something to tell Anike,' Yannick said to his wife, 'if she starts talking about Christian only treating rich patients so he can line his pockets with their fees.'

'Oh, she's not serious when she says that,' Irène returned.

Christian turned to her.

'So you'll be coming to us on Tuesday in preparation for the event?' he asked.

'Well . . . actually I'm not so sure.' Irène winced as she spoke.

'You mean—?'

'Yes, I think it's starting now,' Irène nodded wryly, making the dramatic statement in as matter-of-fact a way as if she had been saying that it was time for the News.

'*Chérie*, why didn't you say?' Yannick was suddenly concerned and pale.

'Because I've only just decided that I'm sure,' Irène replied. 'I wonder if it will be as fast as Marie-Laure. She came in less than an hour from start to finish.'

'Good heavens, yes, she did too!' Christian was already on his feet.

'What's wrong with Maman?' asked Laurent, beginning to look worried as he grasped that something was happening.

'Our new baby is going to be born, darling,' Irène told him, summoning a smile, though Madeleine could see that already the pain was coming more frequently and strongly.

'I'll take the children round to Lucien and Henriette's,' Yannick said.

He rose from the table and organised the departure of the two little ones with quiet efficiency, capturing their co-operation with promises of games with their cousins, and the excitement of an overnight stay at his brother Lucien's house.

Christian questioned Irène carefully about how she was feeling, while Madeleine quietly began to clear the remains of the meal into the kitchen. The surgeon stopped her after a minute.

'I'm going down to bring my car round,' he told her. 'I'll be back in a few minutes to get Irène. We'll go to the local hospital. Can you help to make her comfortable until then?'

'Of course.'

He disappeared immediately, leaving the two women alone in the apartment.

'Do you want to sit down?' Madeleine asked Irène.

'No, I'd rather keep moving,' the older woman said. 'This is just how it was with Marie-Laure.' For a minute she said nothing, then spoke again. 'I have a horrible feeling that Christian is wasting his time going to get the car. I think it's too late to get to the hospital.'

'Do you mean that?' Madeleine asked urgently.

'Ummm . . .' The hesitation turned into an expression of pain. 'Yes.'

'Then this table is probably the best place for you.'

Madeleine wasted no time. She bundled the remaining items from the table into the cloth that had covered it and took the parcel into the kitchen, dumping it unceremoniously on the sink, fortunately without breaking anything. Next she began to boil water, and with Irène's help, found clean linen and pillows that could be used for support.

The door of the apartment banged and Christian strode in.

'Irène, are you . . .'

'I'm not going, Christian,' she said. 'It's too late. I know this feeling from the time with Marie-Laurie. The contractions are coming so fast now . . .'

Christian took in the situation at a glance.

'You may well be almost in second stage. Do you feel that you want to bear down yet?'

'No.'

'Good, then we have a bit of time. Madeleine, there are a few more things I'll need. I know this apartment, so

I'll find them. I see you've started to prepare everything.'

'Yes, I've done a few things. There hasn't been much time.'

'No, you've done a good job. Can you look after Irène now, while I get my bag from the car and make the rest of the preparations?'

'Yes, Doctor.'

It felt as though they were in theatre together, and Madeleine realised that they had never worked so closely with each other before. She wished she had time just to observe him—the way his face was set in concentration, betraying the rapid thought processes that were taking place; the way not one movement of his long lithe body was a wasted one, and the way he managed to find time to toss an encouraging smile or word to Irène whenever he was in the room.

After gathering various things, he returned to his car to get the black medical bag he always carried. Madeleine helped Irène to undress and put on a roomy nightgown which would be comfortable yet at the same time not impede the process of the birth. Some time passed, during which the frequency and pain of the contractions grew stronger, then Irène was already to lie down, fully supported by the pillows on the table top, whose hard surface and greater height would be much easier to work on than a bed.

Madeleine had spent only three months in an obstetrics ward during her time at St Catherine's, but it had been an area that had always interested her, so she had worked particularly hard there, and felt a sense of challenge but not fear, now, about the task that lay ahead.

'I feel as though I want to push now,' Irène said, well

in control with her breathing, although she gave low groans each time the pain of a contraction seized her again.

'Yes, you seem to be fully dilated,' Madeleine nodded.

'Is Christian going to come?'

'Do you want him?'

'Yes.'

There was a note of panic in Irène's voice now as the birth was imminent. She had been very lucky in that she was one of those women who have a quick, smooth labour, but these final minutes would still be an ordeal. Madeleine saw that beads of perspiration stood out on Irène's forehead now, and her face was creased and red with intense effort.

Christian had returned now, breathing heavily, as he had obviously run down and up the three flights of stairs without waiting for the lift. He went to the bathroom and scrubbed up quickly. Irène couldn't stop herself from crying out now, and gripping Madeleine's arm as she stood at the side of the table.

'It will be very soon now,' said Christian, his manner a mixture of warm support and the efficiency of a surgeon.

Irène was by now past caring that it was her own brother who was helping her with the birth. Madeleine looked at Christian and suspected that he had forgotten the fact too, as minutes ticked past and all three of them were completely absorbed in Irène's effort.

A quick check with Christian's stethoscope assured him that the baby's heartbeat rate was normal and the head was strongly engaged now. Irène was responding fully to her urge to bear down, and Madeleine could see that it would be just a few more minutes before the baby was born.

'Do I need to prepare for an episiotomy?' Madeleine asked.

'No. We're lucky—she's not going to tear. There should be no problems at all,' said Christian. 'In fact, it's coming now.'

Gently, but with insistent pressure, he took hold of the head and drew it out, then helped the tiny body to rotate ninety degrees to bring the shoulders through, and coaxed the remainder of the baby's body into the world.

'It's a boy,' Madeleine said gently to Irène, who was already more relaxed and in less pain.

Dr Galantière was continuing with his work, cutting the umbilical cord and checking that the baby was ready to breathe. So far he had made no sound, then suddenly cries came for a moment, and he was breathing normally.

When Yannick returned half an hour later, having been on a wild-goose chase to the hospital, he was astounded to find that everything was over. The seven-pound boy had been cleaned of virnex and dried carefully, and was now resting beside his mother. The afterbirth had been safely delivered, and Irene could now relax fully in a second clean nightdress.

'You mean I've missed it all?' Yannick demanded incredulously.

'I'm afraid so,' Christian laughed. He was still taking care of the final cleaning and tidying operations as he spoke, but he looked very happy.

'That's . . . incredible. Irène?' Yannick turned to his tired wife and they clung to each other for a moment, practically smothering the sleeping baby.

Madeleine turned away, feeling suddenly on the verge of tears, and wanting to leave Irène and Yannick to their private moment together. Tonight had been different from the births she had witnessed and assisted with at St Catherine's. There, they had all involved strangers, and Madeleine herself had been only the most junior member of the medical team. Tonight, though, her contribution had been important, and she had shared it with Christian. That fact ought not to affect her at all—ought, if anything, to make her feel awkward and tense, yet she did not.

The whole experience had passed like a whirlwind, and she knew that her memories of it would be only confused ones, but the feeling that remained with her now was one of deep happiness, and she could not separate Christian's presence from that, though she did not understand why.

'Madeleine.' He spoke to her now, stepping towards her. She blinked away the traces of tears quickly and smiled up at him. 'I still have a few things to do. Irène ought to get into a proper bed as soon as possible. She'll be tired out and will want to sleep. Would you like to make the bed up in the bedroom with fresh sheets and arrange a table by the bed with anything that she may need on it?'

'Of course.'

Madeleine began to move away, wanting to do so because she was far too aware of his nearness. He was so tall that her eyes only came level with his chest, and she found herself looking at the neat hollow below his neck at the point where his collarbone made a V. His skin was very soft and brown there. It was the kind of place that she would like to snuggle up to for comfort . . .

No! That was not the way to think. It was far too dangerous. Hadn't she already determined quite firmly that her physical attraction to him and her memory of his kiss was not going to affect the dislike of him that was her only defence?

'Madeleine,' he spoke softly. 'Wait.'

He looked over and saw that Yannick and Irène were still completely absorbed in each other and in their new child. Madeleine was forced to look up and meet his insistent gaze, and her knees went weak. Reaction was beginning to set in after the dramatic events of the last two hours, and again she felt like crying, but willed the tears to stay dammed behind her eyes.

Christian reached out an arm and pulled her close to him. It was not a kiss, but fire ran through her as much as if it had been.

'You were exceptional,' he told her. 'I couldn't have asked for more support. I was so glad you were here.'

Madeleine could not think of a reply. It was too achingly pleasant to feel the heat of his arm and the support of his chest pressed against her. She wanted to burrow her face into the hollow of his shoulder and stay there for minutes, breathing the warm scent of musk that surrounded him.

But she must not do that. His touch was merely the acknowledgment that they had performed well as a team. It was a gesture of comradeship that you could see among sportsmen in a field, not the caress of a lover.

She broke away—so reluctantly, but very firmly.

'I'm quite tired,' she said with a shaky laugh. 'I had no strength then for a moment. Sorry. I'll go and make up that bed now.'

'Do you know where the sheets are kept?' His voice was as controlled and matter-of-fact as her own.

'Yes, I found them earlier. There are still several clean ones, although I used two on the table.'

'Good . . .' Christian's manner had suddenly become

abstracted again. Probably the way they had just touched each other had already passed out of his thoughts. Madeleine suppressed a sigh, and went to do as he had asked her.

When Irène was safely settled in the freshly-made bed with her baby beside her, and everything in the apartment tidied and returned to normal, Christian came out from the kitchen with a tray of tea things. Yannick and Irène drank theirs in the bedroom, while Christian and Madeleine sat in the dining room, saying very little. Madeleine noted absently that it was dark outside, which it had not been before.

'What's the time?' she asked.

'What do you think?' Christian countered with a smile, after consulting his watch.

'I have no idea,' Madeleine replied. 'As far as my instincts go, it could be seven in the evening or three in the morning.'

'Exactly halfway in between.'

'What are we . . . what's happening next?' she asked.

'What would you like to do?' Christian returned. 'Has the tea revived you? Could you bear to drive back to Le Breuil tonight? Or would you prefer to find a hotel here?'

'You would prefer to go back, wouldn't you?'

'That's not the point,' he said. 'I'm asking what you would like to do?'

Madeleine thought of the last time they had stayed at a hotel together, and how much promise that had seemed to hold. So little remained of that now. It would be safer to get this unexpected time with Christian over with as quickly as possible, before he took possession of her senses and her heart even more than he had already done.

'I'd rather go back. I've . . . I've made an arrangement with Julie Rondin for tomorrow,' she lied. 'We
both have the day off.'

'Very well,' he nodded. 'We'll start as soon as possible, then. I'd just like to ring Irène's doctor here in
Marseille to tell her what has happened and ask her to
check on Irène first thing in the morning.'

'Of course.'

He left the room, to return a few minutes later, having
successfully made the call.

'Irène is asleep now,' he said. 'She seems to be
progressing very well. Everything is perfectly normal,
and the baby is fine. Yannick is going to sit up with him
for a few hours, but I can't imagine that anything will go
wrong. I think we can go.'

Madeleine stood up and looked about, feeling that she
had been here for such a long time and so much had
happened that surely she ought to have some luggage to
take away. There was only her handbag, of course, and
the lacy crocheted cardigan she had brought to wear
over her yellow dress. It was incredible to think that
she had only been in this apartment for a little over six
hours.

They walked out together into the night, which
Madeleine found cool and refreshing after the warmth
that had built up in the apartment.

It was two by the time they arrived at Le Breuil, and
the hospital building was dark in most places and very
quiet. Madeleine had dozed during the journey and
Christian had not spoken. Now he came to a gentle stop
in his usual parking spot and touched her softly on the
shoulder.

'We're home. Are you awake?'

'Just.'

'Before you go . . . may I ask you to do something for me?'

'Of course,' she nodded, feeling wide awake now.

'Don't say anything about all this to the rest of the staff. People will know soon, of course, that my sister has had her baby, but Irène is a fairly private person, and she might not want the whole of Le Breuil knowing exactly how it all happened,' Christian said.

'That's understandable,' Madeleine nodded. 'It will be very easy for me to say nothing about it.'

'I'd be grateful. Now you'd better go and get a good sleep.'

'Yes, I'm sure I need one.' Madeleine remembered how the day had started—such a long time ago, it seemed—and the pleasant afternoon she had had with Richard. 'Thank you so much for driving me to Marseille. It was a . . . well, it was a very enjoyable day.'

'You don't have to say that,' said Christian. 'I'm the one who has to thank you, for Irène and Yannick's sake as well as my own.'

He paused and drew in a breath as if he was about to say more, but then was silent after all. Madeleine looked at him for a moment, trying not to see black eyes that were like deep pools, smooth dark skin and curls that were endearingly disarrayed after the long day. She wished he would frown at her, or brush her off with some curt comment, but he did not, and she knew she would have to leave the car of her own accord before her longing for him grew too great.

'Good night, Dr Galantière.'

'Good night.'

Madeleine could not resist pausing halfway along the maze of corridors at a window that looked out from the second floor over the gravel driveway. Christian would be walking to the extended wing at the end of which was his own four-roomed apartment—a place she would probably never see inside.

Yes, there he was, a tall figure that could only dimly be picked out of the darkness on this moonless night. The pale blue shirt he wore was the only part of him that was clearly visible. As Madeleine looked, she saw that he had stopped and turned back to look up at the hospital. She drew back to the edge of the window, although she was sure he would not be able to see her. This corridor was particularly dark, and there was no light behind her to create a silhouette.

What could he be looking at? Perhaps he had heard a noise in the building, or seen a new light come on somewhere in one of the wards, and was wondering if everything was all right. Now he had begun to walk again, and in another few seconds had disappeared along the shrub-lined path that led to his door.

Madeleine continued on her way feeling suddenly depressed. Anticlimax after the drama of the day, of course. The fact that images of Christian would not fade from her mind's eye had nothing to do with it at all.

CHAPTER SEVEN

IT was rather a relief for Madeleine to find herself back on Hibiscus Ward on Wednesday morning. She had spent her next two days off pleasantly but quietly after the dramatic events of Sunday, lazing on the beach with Julie for most of Monday, and spending Tuesday by herself. She had caught a series of local buses that wound through the villages to the north of the coast, getting off every now and then to explore a small church or enjoy a drink at an outdoor café.

But through all this it had been difficult to dismiss Christian Galantière from her mind. Being involved so closely in the birth of Irène's baby had brought them together in a way that might have been important if there had not been such a gulf between them. Madeleine did not know whether to look forward to seeing him on the ward, or to dread further contact.

And how was he feeling? It was impossible to know. Her own confused emotions clouded her usual sensitivity to other people, and she found the surgeon as unreadable as if he had been a complete stranger. Plunging herself into the work of nursing would force her to think of other things, she decided, and distract her from musings which were circular, negative and exhausting.

There were several new patients this week, most being prepared for or recovering from routine surgery. An old man occupied the bed that Patrice had had during Madeleine's first two days on the ward. The sixty-five-year-old colostomy patient reminded Madeleine in many ways of the much younger fair-haired playboy.

Monsieur Perrotin seemed quite reconciled to the operation he had had on Monday, facing philosophically the differences it would make to his life and his daily routine, and already cheerful though still in pain.

'I haven't seen you before,' he said to Madeleine when she came to check his progress and make some routine observations on Wednesday morning.

'I've just had three days off,' Madeleine explained.

'You're not French, are you?' he asked, just as Patrice had done the first time she had spoken to him.

'No, I'm English,' Madeleine replied with a smile.

'I see. Here to look after our tourists?'

'Sometimes, yes.'

'Well, I hope they don't spirit you off to another ward while I'm here,' Monsieur Perrotin said. 'I have a feeling that seeing your face smiling at me as you fiddle with all those wretched instruments and contraptions will make me feel better a lot quicker.'

Madeleine could not help laughing, as Patrice had so often made her do. She had not seen him since he had roared off in his Jaguar on Sunday morning. That was only three days ago, but it seemed much longer because of how full and long that Sunday had been. Madeleine did not know if he was angry with her for not going to Marseille with him, but hoped he was not.

She did not want to lose the friendship that they had begun to build. She remembered how both Tanya Garcia and Julie Rondin had assumed that it was more than friendship—or that, at any rate, Patrice would like it to be. Were they right? Madeleine did not know, but wondered what her reaction would be if he became insistent.

She liked him very much most of the time. Was it a feeling that could grow stronger with time, and with seeing more of him? She thought unwillingly of Christian, then was angry with herself. He had nothing to do with it. Admittedly, she was attracted to the man, but nothing could come of it, so it was quite irrelevant to think of him and Patrice together, or to make any kind of comparison between them.

Madeleine was conscious, however, that she very often kept half an eye out for Christian's appearance on the ward, even though his routine was fairly fixed now that things were back to normal after his three weeks in England.

He usually did not appear on the ward until three to check those patients who had had surgery that morning, so if Madeleine was working a morning shift, which she was rostered to do for the next two weeks apart from a couple of days off, she had little chance of seeing him, Probably it was just as well.

Madeleine decided firmly, as she answered another mischievous comment from Monsieur Perrotin, that a phone call from Patrice was the thing she would look forward to.

It came four days later on Sunday evening, exactly a week since the birth of Irène's baby. In that time, Madeleine had spoken to Christian only once. On one of his rare visits to the dining room, he had stopped by her table to say quietly that Irène and her baby were continuing to do well, and that they wanted to convey their thanks again for their help. Madeleine had nodded and murmured a polite nothing, then Fabienne had come to the table with her tray, so the surgeon had moved on. Apart from that, Madeleine had seen Christian only in the distance as he made his way around the hospital—as busy as ever with many tasks and problems. Once they had passed in a corridor and had nodded briefly in greeting, but that was all. Naturally he made no attempt to seek out her company.

Patrice's caressing and mischievous voice at the other end of the telephone line was very welcome.

'I rang you yesterday morning, too, actually,' he said evidently pleased at the warmth in her voice as she greeted him.

'I didn't hear about that!'

'No, I know. I told them not to bother to give you a message. They said you were working. Whenever I want to take you boating you seem to be working,' he complained.

'Oh, did you want to take me boating?' Madeleine was disappointed.

'Yes, my love. An overnight yachting cruise with Tanya and Serge Garcia, and some American friends. Perhaps you might know them—the Phyffers,' he said.

'The name doesn't sound familiar. Why did you think I might know them?'

'Oh, friends in common,' Patrice replied vaguely.

'Really? I know almost no Americans.'

To her surprise he laughed, but then changed the subject.

'When are you free?' he asked.

'It depends what you mean by free,' she replied. 'I work early shifts tomorrow and Tuesday, which means I finish at three and am free for the rest of the day, although I like to get to bed fairly early as I'm usually tired. Then I have Wednesday off.'

'You nurses! What uncivilised hours you keep. I don't know how you stick it, Madeleine.'

'I like it,' she replied. 'I like the work, and working

odd hours keeps you on your toes. Besides, what would you suggest I did to make a living?'

Again he laughed and did not reply to the question.

'May I call for you tomorrow?' he asked. 'We'll go for a drive and perhaps a swim—I have a feeling it's going to be hot. Then we could eat together. There's a restaurant in Le Breuil that is quite nice. Not at all *chic*, but the food is good, if that is enough for you.'

'Naturally it is,' said Madeleine. 'I don't care anything at all about what's *chic*. Tomorrow would be lovely.'

'Can you be ready by half past three?'

'Yes, that would be just right.'

The next day, the promise of the outing added zest to her work, although it was a busy day and she was late finishing. She encountered Dr Galantière in the corridor just as she was pulling off her cap and shaking out her fluffy black hair after leaving the ward. It was almost half past three, and the surgeon was on his way to see his patients.

Madeleine felt able to give him a confident smile after her enjoyable day, and he actually returned it, and stopped to speak. Perhaps the way they had worked together in Marseille had made a faint impression on him after all.

'You look cheerful,' he remarked. 'Are you on your way somewhere?'

'Yes, for a drive and a swim, and perhaps dinner.'

'Ah, of course. With Patrice de Brabant. That must have been his car I just heard pulling up outside.'

His manner had turned frosty again and he continued on his way. Madeleine was annoyed. The antagonism between the surgeon and Patrice was no secret to her. Christian must know that. He must also know that she was friends with the young financier. Surely it was her business if she saw him socially? Or did Dr Galantière think that he had the right to regulate who his staff saw in their free time?

Madeleine seized gladly on this chance to feel hostile to the French surgeon and fumed determinedly as she hurried along the corridors and stairways towards her little white room. Christian had indicated that Patrice was already waiting for her, and she still had to change and gather her things.

Madeleine checked as she passed the window that faced out on to the driveway. Yes, there he was, pacing around the gravel in front of the main entrance, a thin wisp of smoke rising from his Turkish cigarette. Fabienne Noyer came out of the foyer and down the steps to greet Patrice enthusiastically. Madeleine smiled. She was becoming quite used to the French nurse's flirtations now, seeing her often at meals or during their coffee breaks, and she didn't really mind it by this time.

When Madeleine returned along the corridor, dressed now in her yellow sundress, with a swimming costume beneath and a towel and straw bag in her hands, Fabienne was still standing with Patrice, who looked less than happy now. Madeleine hoped he was not becoming angry with her lateness. She hurried down.

Fabienne had gone when she arrived, and Patrice had begun a second cigarette. He looked up when he saw her approach, his green eyes narrowed.

'I'm so sorry I'm late, Patrice,' she apologised. 'I had to stay extra time on the ward. I was in the middle of something and couldn't leave it.'

She expected him to make some tease, or forgive her with a quick kiss, but he did not.

'I can't take you out after all,' he said shortly, offering

no apology. 'Something's come up. What a mistake! I should have realised . . . God, how ridiculous!'

'Why? What is it? Is it your work? Has something gone wrong?'

'I'm afraid I couldn't possibly explain,' said Patrice with an intonation of grim humour.

'Well, I hope you sort it all out,' Madeleine said. She was very confused by his manner; it was unlike anything she had seen in him before. 'Will you ring me and we can arrange another time?'

'Yes, soon,' Patrice promised absently, but he was frowning and she sensed that he had not really been listening. She could not help feeling hurt. She had been looking forward to the afternoon with Patrice, and now he did not even seem particularly regretful that it could not happen.

He was already walking back to his low car, not even bothering to ask her how she was, or make any of the teasing comments that she had grown to enjoy from him. If he was going to be so cool about the whole thing, why hadn't he simply rung her to say that he was cancelling their outing?

Over the next week she heard nothing from him, and though she tried to tell herself that it wasn't important and that she did not care, it was difficult not to feel her pride and sense of self-worth slightly dinted by the inexplicable episode.

It was not until the following Monday that Madeleine understood what it had all been about.

As often happened, Madeleine found that Julie and Fabienne were in the shared coffee-making area of the nurses' station when she went in there for her morning break, after beginning work at seven. It was also quite usual that she should talk with Julie while Fabienne read a cheap magazine, looking up occasionally to comment about the doings of some starlet whom neither Julie nor Madeleine were particularly interested in.

It was fortunate, Madeleine had thought more than once, that Fabienne's obsession with glittering news-makers was tempered with an earthy kind of common sense in many areas, which meant that she never got too painfully caught up in her fantasies.

'Now here's a photo of someone who nearly got me into a lot of trouble,' she commented, putting down a half-finished cup of coffee, and shaking her blonde head ruefully. 'Come and look, Madeleine. You're going to laugh at me.'

'Really? Why?' Madeleine queried, putting her own tea-cup down and crossing the small space to look over Fabienne's shoulder at the place where she had her finger on the magazine.

There was a photo, taken by flash-bulb at some New York nightclub, of a very wealthy and glamorous-looking young woman. She was not exactly beautiful, but she had an interesting and lively face. Unfortunately Madeleine had no idea who she was, and so could not respond to Fabienne's comment in the proper vein.

'Who is she?' she asked.

'Look at the caption: Madelyn Caine, heiress to the Sagatex oil empire, seems unperturbed by photo-graphers at the opening of Stir 90, the fashionable new nightclub, etcetera, etcetera. The point is, I thought she was you. You see, she was reported missing several weeks ago, just about the time when you arrived. I was reading about it in a magazine in this very room. They said she had trained as a nurse in England—to have a career to fall back on, I suppose. Your name was so similar, I thought you were just disguising your real one.

And the description of her—see, she's very dark. They said she had gone into hiding to rethink her life after some affair had broken up. You looked a bit miserable when you first came. I put two and two together—or so I thought—and was quite sure you were her. Don't I have a vivid imagination?' Fabienne finished with an unconcerned laugh. Madeleine was speechless.

'I should think you do!' Julie was saying, having listened open-mouthed to this tale as well. 'The only thing that amazes me is that you managed to keep the whole thing a secret, and didn't pester Madeleine with it night and day. It would have been much more like you to spread the story over the whole hospital and have everyone believing it.'

'Well, I did tell one person,' Fabienne admitted. 'And he told me that the idea was nonsense, so then I forgot about it.'

'Really? Who was that?' asked Julie.

'Patrice de Brabant. I was cross. I thought he'd be interested, but he rubbished the idea, then when I found out the other day that he was right and told him so, he seemed furious, as if he had believed my theory all along after all,' Fabienne explained.

The implications of what she was saying did not seem to have occurred to her, but they had certainly not escaped Madeleine's awareness. Julie turned to her now.

'What about you, Madeleine, what do you think? You are the one that's most concerned in all this, and you haven't said anything.'

'I don't know what to say,' she managed to reply.

It was the truth. Her head was awhirl. Quite a few things were suddenly clear to her, and they shed a very ugly light on Patrice. It was obvious that he *had* believed

Fabienne, but had rubbished the idea so that she would say nothing more about it, and he could be free to claim Madeleine's attention—and eventually her trust and love—for himself. Beneath his apparent and frank interest in her had been a far more calculating level that horrified her.

She remembered several things he had said to try and coax her to confess her supposed true identity, and she remembered his evasiveness about his work. Was he just an out-and-out gigolo? She could not quite believe that. Probably he made a certain amount of money through business interests—whether legitimate or illegitimate, she would not hazard a guess—but obviously the thought of coasting through an easy future with someone else's money to spend had appealed to him quite a bit, and he had been prepared to spend money and time, and to go slowly with his lovemaking, in order to capture her deepest affections.

Then the other day when he had been about to take her out and had said suddenly that he could not—he had been talking to Fabienne just before that. It must have been then that the French nurse had laughingly told him of her mistake. To her the whole thing had been part of the frothy fantasy world that she entertained herself with in spare moments, but to Patrice it had been something more serious.

As she put these facts together, Madeleine thought that it seemed like a very dramatic explanation, but she was sure it was the right one, and she knew she would not hear from Patrice again.

'You're not cross, are you?' asked Fabienne. 'After all, it has only shown up my silliness. You haven't suffered at all.'

'No, I haven't,' Madeleine agreed.

Was it true? For a moment, anger and damaged pride seethed inside her. Patrice had never liked her for herself at all. It had been her mythical fortune and nothing else. She might have been badly hurt.

Then she knew that she was not, and realised that Patrice had never touched her heart. She had enjoyed his company when she believed him to be an uncomplicated fun-loving man, but now that she knew the truth, she could feel sorry for him, put the affair down to experience, and relegate it to the past. No deeper feelings were involved.

'We'd better get back to work,' Julie was saying now in a cross voice. 'We've wasted enough time over this stupid thing.'

'Stupid?' Fabienne looked at her, flushed, and a little hurt.

'Well, I suppose it is only a joke, really,' Julie laughed, but Madeleine caught a quick anxious glance directed at herself.

'She knows what Patrice was up to,' Madeleine realised. 'Or at least suspects, and she's worried that I've been hurt. She's a real friend.'

Julie found an opportunity to speak to Madeleine that evening after dinner.

'Patrice thought you had money, and that's why he was taking you out, isn't it?' she asked with concern.

'Yes, I've realised that too,' Madeleine laughed.

'You're not upset?'

'Not really. I'm glad I found out in time, but I don't think I could ever have got serious about him. We just aren't concerned about the same things, and I knew that even before Fabienne made her confession this morning.'

'I'm glad. I've never liked him all that much,' said

Julie with an odd intonation. 'I didn't want to say that before, when I thought you might be falling in love with him. He . . . used to hang around the hospital quite a bit at one stage. He's fun, I admit, but I think he can also be dangerous.'

But despite Madeleine's assurance to Julie and her own inner conviction, Madeleine did feel a little desolate in the week that followed. It was never nice to feel that you had been tricked and betrayed, and Madeleine started to wonder if all the men she met at Le Breuil were going to be very different on closer acquaintance from how she had first perceived them. There had been Christian Galantière—cold, then too warm, and now so distant again as well as Patrice.

Work on the ward continued to be very satisfying, however. Madeleine spent three days on Women's Surgical, where there was an Englishwoman who was very distressed after a road accident and had to have over a dozen pieces of shattered glass removed from her arms and face by surgery. Madeleine was able to explain hospital procedure in France, and help the woman find out about her travel insurance policy.

She enjoyed returning to Hibiscus Ward, however, as of all the Sisters with whom she worked, calm but cheerful Sister Angèle was her favourite.

Monsieur Perrotin continued to be a source of pleasure as well as anxiety, too. His condition improved rapidly, but he was almost too eager to pass each new stage of convalescence, and was becoming very impatient with his own inactivity. Madeleine had to calm him down and restrain him several times when he tried to do things that he was simply not yet ready for, and yet she was sympathetic to his feelings.

'Look at this glorious weather!' he would say. 'I run a

boat business off Antibes. I love being out there, with the sea and the salt in the air. June and July are my favourite months, and I'm spending them cooped up in here, worrying that my son is not handling the business right. Why couldn't this have happened in winter when I didn't want to spend every minute of the day out in the sun and wind, and when business falls off? I'm furious!'

'If you're not careful, your impatience will keep you in here a lot longer,' Madeleine warned him.

'How is that?'

'You're not yet ready to be active. You have to rest your body, let it get accustomed to what has happened, otherwise you could strain your whole system.'

'And what could happen?'

'Infection, haemorrhage, heart trouble.'

He nodded and became more sober, but still could not let himself rest as he should. Of course, the very fact that he was optimistic and still prepared to enjoy life was in his favour, but Madeleine felt anxious all the same.

She was to remember her warning to him two days later on Sunday afternoon. She was in charge of this shift, as it was usually a quiet one. Any urgent operations that were performed were sent to intensive care, so patients on Hibiscus Ward were recovering from surgery that had taken place no more recently than Friday, and were all in a stable condition. Any patients who were to have surgery on Monday were admitted later in the afternoon, when the next set of nurses came on to the ward.

It was at one, about fifteen minutes after Madeleine had returned from her lunch break, that the junior nurse, Simone Pézet, came up to her, looking very white.

'The colostomy patient in bed eighteen, Sister Carver. He has died!'

'Monsieur Perrotin? Oh no!' Madeleine felt sick and faint, but made herself stand firm.

It was a thing most nurses dreaded, yet knew that they would have to face once in a while. No matter how old or ill a patient was, no matter how little could have been done to save them, and how predictable their death was, it was always a shock, and left a sense of sadness and regret.

Madeleine was not wasting time, however. She walked quickly to Monsieur Perrotin's bed and asked Sister Pézet to put up a screen. Both women acted as calmly as possible, not wanting to disturb or arouse the curiosity of the other patients. Madeleine bent over the inert form of the man whom she had been slowly growing fond of. Yes, there was no doubt.

His face was pale and peaceful, betraying that unearthliness which can never be described or captured. He looked as if he had died very easily—in his sleep, perhaps, with no warning to himself that it was coming.

'It must have been his heart,' Madeleine murmured, her own beating painfully.

'You'll have to call Dr Galantière, won't you, to sign the certificate,' said Sister Pézet. 'Monsieur Perrotin was his patient.'

'Yes, I know.' Madeleine pulled herself together and straightened up, trying to block out useless regrets by becoming brisk and thinking efficiently. 'He'll want to know straight away. I'll go down to his office. He may not be there, of course, but I can try. If not, perhaps he is in his apartment.'

She was speaking just for the sake of it. Words helped.

'I'll be all right by myself here. It's a very quiet day,' Sister Pézet assured her.

'Of course you will.'

Madeleine left the ward, and the thoughts she had tried to repress came flooding in. Perhaps there was something she could have done . . . Should she have monitored his condition more carefully? Warned him more seriously about the dangers of over-exerting himself? Told Dr Galantière about his patient's attitude? If it had been some other surgeon in charge, might not she have done so?

Perhaps it was only because she avoided speaking to Christian Galantière wherever possible that. she had not.

Madeleine knew that this sense of crushing responsibility always came. But this time perhaps it was her fault. And she had to go to Dr Galantière and tell him.

He was in his office. She could hear the sound of a filing drawer closing, then his swivel chair creaked. He answered the door several seconds after her knock. Madeleine had barely seen him over the past week; their schedules simply had not coincided. Now, even with her emotions agitated by poor Monsieur Perrotin's death, she could not be completely impervious to the surgeon's impressive presence.

It was, for once, a cool day, so he wore a sleeveless Fair-Isle pullover in grey, maroon and cream over a loose-sleeved white shirt that was teamed with well-tailored grey wool pants. The shirt was open at the neck, as it often was when he worked. As well, Madeleine could see by the way his hair lay in loose tangles, that he had been passing an abstracted hand through it in his usual gesture.

'Sister Carver! What can I do for you?'

He smiled as if he was actually pleased to see her, but probably it was merely that he was struggling with administrative problems, and any interruption was welcome.

Madeleine thought of what she had come to say, and of how difficult it was to say it to this man, and suddenly she found she was trembling, and had to grit her teeth to keep control. He must have sensed that something was wrong, as he put an arm gently round her shoulders, pushed the door shut softly with the flat of his other hand and ushered her in.

His touch was too much, and tears had already started to her eyes as she began to speak.

'Monsieur Perrotin, I think it must have been his heart. He did just a few minutes ago . . . peacefully. You'll have to—'

She couldn't go on, feeling a sob rise against her will and control.

It wasn't simply Monsieur Perrotin, it was Christian, the concern she saw reflected in his dark eyes and the soft frown that creased his brow, and it was Father and Jean all over again, and Richard so far away . . .

'Shh . . . shhh!'

She was folded against him now, her ear pressed against the soft wool that covered his chest. She could hear his heartbeat, and the soothing sounds he made vibrating in his diaphragm. He held one hand around her shoulders, kneading them softly, while the other played caressingly through the curls which had escaped her cap in the nape of her neck.

But she knew that it was not she, Madeleine Carver, who was arousing such a caring response in him. He was a doctor, he had cared for three younger sisters, he was a man who loved and understood children. This kind of reaction came automatically from him when he saw someone in tears.

She was about to pull away, but she felt him loosen his own hold, so she relaxed, thinking that he was going to end the moment, but instead he had lifted her chin with gentle fingers and found her lips. His kiss was urgent and demanding, and his mouth was firm and warm. Madeleine was awash with turbulent feeling, needing to respond fully even though she knew she must not. All sense of time and space disappeared for her, and her eyes were closed. This could go on for ever . . .

But it must not. She knew from her past experience with this man that he meant nothing by it. Perhaps, again, it was a gesture designed to comfort her in some way, as his gentle arms about her a moment ago had been. Whatever his reasons for initiating their kiss, they could not be the same as her reasons for responding.

'Madeleine . . .'

'I'm all right now.' She eased herself away and reached into the pocket of her uniform for a handkerchief, deliberately making the gesture as unromantic as possible. 'Sorry, that was stupid. I've finished crying. You'd better go up to the ward. If you don't mind, I'll just stop off at a washroom and splash my face a bit.'

He opened his mouth to speak, but at that moment a knock came at the door, and Madeleine heard a gay voice outside. Christian's call of 'Come in!' was irritated and tense until the door opened and Irène stood there with her three-week-old baby in her arms and Yannick just behind her.

'We've paid you a surprise visit,' she said, laughing. She had not yet caught sight of Madeleine with her tear-stained face. 'I hope you don't mind. Laurent and Marie-Laure are with Lucien and Henriette, but we thought you'd like to see your namesake. Christian, see your big uncle!'

She broke off, noticing both Madeleine and her tears at the same moment. Christian saw her reaction and said quickly:

'It's all right, Irène. An elderly patient has just died on Madeleine's ward.' His tone was gentle but matter-of-fact. 'I'll have to go and see about it—he was one of my patients.'

'Oh, Christian, I'm sorry!' Irène exclaimed.

'Would you mind waiting here for a while? Madeleine, come back to the ward whenever you feel ready.'

Madeleine watched him as he left, then saw that Irène's gaze was fixed on her.

'She's guessed.' The thought came involuntarily to her. Guessed what? The answer was suddenly surprisingly obvious: that Madeleine was in love with Christian.

It was a stunning revelation of her own feelings and it left Madeleine weak, very thankful that she had a chair to sink into for support. How long had this feeling been at the root of all her confusion about the French surgeon? All along, probably. Even during that first unfortunate meeting at his hotel in London when he had been so hostile.

On their drive down to Le Breuil she had begun to consciously recognise the feeling within herself, but when he had suddenly turned so cold she had talked herself out of it and really begun to believe that she disliked him. Then her day in Marseille had shown her a new side to his personality which she had instinctively responded to.

Now she knew she could no longer convince herself of

her dislike, even though their relationship was as hopeless as it had ever been. Perhaps she *should* still dislike him. After all, the reasons she had found to do so before still held. He had flirted with her then rejected her, had used his kiss with no thought of what it might do to her. But she could not dislike him. The times when he was charming outweighed the coldness she did not understand . . .

What was she going to do about this new understanding of her feelings? She did not yet know. The speed and suddenness with which the whole thing had happened left her totally confused. There was only one thing that was clear at the moment. Christian Galantière must not be allowed to suspect, and that meant wiping any trace of her feelings from her face now, so that Irène did not have the chance to read the truth there unmistakably.

'Do you want to go and wash your face, Madeleine?' Irène was asking with concern.

'No, I'm all right now, I think,' Madeleine replied, summoning a smile. She did not care if her tears showed, but was terrified that Christian's kiss might still be evident there in her expression, or in the slight disarray of her hair. 'Is my face very red?'

'No, it's not too bad at all,' Yannick put in.

'May I look at little Christian?' Madeleine asked Irène.

'Of course. After all, you were one of the first people to see him. But hasn't he changed and grown already?'

He had. Madeleine remembered a tiny wrinkled creature with a face so red it was almost purple, and damp sticky hair clinging to its little scalp. Now he was smooth and serene, not asleep for the moment but gazing about with interested though slightly unfocused brown eyes. His skin was scented with a faint sweetness, and so delicate and fine that it was almost transparent. His curled fingers were impossibly small, yet every part of them perfectly formed.

'He's beautiful,' Madeleine smiled, her absorption in this new life helping her to forget the sadness of the passing of a life upstairs on Hibiscus Ward, and the moment of passion between herself and Christian.

'We've brought you a little present,' said Yannick, when Madeleine had passed little Christian back to his mother. 'To thank you for everything you did that night.'

'Oh no! Why? You shouldn't have,' Madeleine exclaimed.

But Yannick insisted on pressing the wrapped parcel into her hands and she opened it to find an enormous assortment of hand-made Russian chocolates that would have her fellow nurses hovering around her for weeks.

'It wasn't at all necessary to thank me with this,' she said. 'But they're beautiful. They look delicious, but they're so prettily packed I'll hardly be able to bear to eat them!'

This comment ended the little scene on a cheerful note, but then Madeleine knew she had to return to the ward. She would never be able to be close friends with Irène and Yannick, although she would have liked to be. They were much too closely linked with Christian, and Madeleine doubted that the tangle of her relationship with him could ever be sorted out now.

CHAPTER EIGHT

MADELEINE struggled painfully into wakefulness and blinked at the clock by her bed. One o'clock. She had been asleep for nearly three hours. It was Saturday night—or rather Sunday morning—and she had worked an early shift that day. Now someone was knocking insistently at her door and calling her name.

More aware of her surroundings now, Madeleine recognised the voice of Dr Galantière. Her heart thumped painfully as ridiculous scenarios flowed through her head. Could he be here because . . . ?

'This isn't a dream, Madeleine Carver,' she told herself angrily, then raised her voice to speak aloud. 'I'm awake—just a minute, please!'

She struggled into her cherry-pink dressing gown and opened the door. Christian stood there fully dressed, his grey jacket covering wool trousers and a pale shirt.

'There's been an accident,' he said urgently. 'I know you're tired, but we're going to need your help. It's a fire in a nightclub in that new resort complex a few miles from here. Most of the people there were apparently English tourists, and we need you to keep them from panicking. Can you be ready and at my car in five minutes?'

'I'll try.'

'Good.'

He strode off down the dark corridor without another word, his manner having been completely impersonal during the entirety of this brief exchange. Madeleine did not waste time, firmly pushing away anything she might have been feeling about seeing Christian here so surprisingly in the middle of the night.

A clean uniform was laid over the back of her chair ready for tomorrow morning's day on the ward. She was soon wearing it, and added thick tights and a jacket as well as her white leather nurse's shoes, because the night was a cool one.

Christian was already in the car and he started the engine as soon as he saw her approach, pulling away from his parking spot before she had even closed the door. He drove faster than she had yet seen him, his face set in tense concentration.

'Tell me more about it, please,' said Madeleine, completely efficient and in control herself, 'so that I'll know exactly what to do when we arrive.'

'We don't know much about it yet,' Christian told her. 'Two ambulances have already left from here with three of our night staff—a doctor and two nurses—co-opted into them. People who were off duty have been called to take their places on the ward. I gather that two ambulances have gone from Antibes, too, but it's likely our own will arrive first. We don't know if they will all be needed. I didn't take the call, but apparently whoever sounded the alarm was pretty panicky.'

'Do you know anything about the nightclub? Have you ever been there?' she asked.

'No, I haven't, but I've heard a bit about it,' the surgeon replied grimly. 'Apparently the whole building was shoddily put together, and the builders took advantage of various loopholes in safety regulations. Your friend Patrice would know more about it than I do. He has some money invested with the company that owns it, and I believe the club is one of his regular hunting grounds. He's never taken you there?'

'No.'

'Perhaps he will in future, if the place hasn't been too badly damaged tonight.'

'I doubt it. I'm not seeing him any more,' Madeleine said shortly. Perhaps it was not the kind of confession she needed to make to Dr Galantière, but she did not care. She stared straight ahead, but saw out of the corner of her eye that Dr Galantière was giving her a searching glance.

'I'm surprised,' he said slowly.

'You needn't be. We were not at all suited to one another.'

Can't you see that it's you I love? Madeleine wanted to say. After Sunday's revelation of her feelings, she wouldn't have wanted to see Patrice again even if he had wanted to see her, and if she had not found out about his real attitude. But what was Christian saying now?

'I can't say I'm sorry that we'll be seeing less of Patrice de Brabant around the hospital,' he said seriously. 'He's not a man I am particularly fond of.'

'Why is that?' Madeleine ventured to ask, thinking suddenly of Patrice making a similar statement that day many weeks ago now when they had driven to Nice together. She had never found out the reason for Patrice's dislike.

'I'll tell you,' the surgeon said slowly. 'Although it's something that only one or two other people at Le Breuil know. Let me just say this. You're not the first nurse at my hospital that Patrice de Brabant has spent time with. He was in for a minor operation about nine months ago and became very friendly with a girl who worked with us then—a good friend of Julie Rondin, but I won't say her name.'

'Is she still at the hospital?'

'No. But she will be spending some time at a hospital in Marseille soon.'

'I'm sorry, I don't . . .'

'Her baby is due in a few weeks.'

Madeleine was stunned into silence, oblivious to the speed of the car as they travelled through quiet streets. Dr Galantière did not have to make his meaning any clearer. She had come across a few women and girls in her work who had been deserted by their child's father, but her picture of the man who would do such a thing had always been very different from the reality of Patrice de Brabant.

She understood Julie's veiled hints too, and the reason for their cryptic nature. Julie was protecting her old friend's confidence, while at the same time trying to warn her new friend against the same fate.

Madeleine came out of her shocked reverie before the surgeon had spoken again, to hear the wail of sirens and see the blaze of lights and flame. She noticed also that they were at the sea-front.

'They've been very lucky,' Christian was saying rapidly. 'Although the nightclub is all part of one complex, with guest rooms and shops, and a number of other facilities, it's here on the waterfront, and is almost separated from the main buildings by a garden restaurant. It may well be only that which has stopped the fire from spreading much further.'

As he spoke he had parked his car, using a few expert motions of the wheel, and finding a place for it which was out of the way of the fire-engines and ambulances, yet at the same time very near to the action. He jumped out of the car and searched for someone official amongst the crowd of helpless tourists and onlookers who were gathered outside.

Madeleine followed, finding it difficult to keep pace with him for a few moments as he dodged expertly between the people. When she arrived at his side he was talking quickly to someone who must be the chief of the fire-fighters. Their conversation was conducted in rapid exchanges of French which Madeleine could not follow above the noise, but Christian turned to her to explain when he finished speaking.

'One ambulance has already left for Le Breuil,' he told her. 'Thank God, I'd already put a stand-by team to work there. Monsieur Trollet here thinks that the best thing for you to do is to move amongst the crowd and find anyone who needs help, especially English-speakers. Apparently the evacuation of the nightclub was chaotic. There was no co-ordination at all, and no-where for people to go for first aid. There will be people amongst this lot who are simply wandering around in shock—perhaps injured without even realising it yet. Try to locate them and help them. Use the first aid supplies in the back of my car. There may not be everything you need—if not, ask one of the ambulance crews for help.'

'Is there somewhere that can be set up quickly as a first-aid station?' asked Madeleine, responding instantly to his clipped, staccato sentences. He was not wasting a word.

'Find somewhere,' he said. 'Talk to one of the fire-fighters, or someone from the management of the complex. Apparently there are a few of them here.'

He was moving away from her as he spoke, taking urgent strides, and Madeleine guessed that the most seriously injured people had already been singled out for his attention. There was no time for her thoughts to dwell on Christian, however.

If she had been able to stand back from the scene and look on it dispassionately, and if someone had told her how much organisation she would succeed in creating out of the chaos, she would not have believed them. But a sense of urgency made so much possible, and all awareness of tiredness was forgotten, as Madeleine worked.

She soon located an official who was connected with the holiday complex, and he turned out to be comparatively calm, unlike the manager, who was wringing his hands and doing nothing constructive at all. Together they arranged for the kitchen of the outdoor restaurant to be opened up and cleared by volunteers for use as an emergency first-aid station.

With its sinks and hot water, it was ideal, although too much of the space was occupied by benches and ovens. The equipment that Dr Galantière had tossed into his car was quickly transferred to the kitchen, where two of the resort complex personnel stayed making hot sweet tea and doing whatever else they could, while Madeleine went out into the crowds in search of injured people.

Dimly she was aware that the flames of the fire were lessening, and that water now drenched the extensively damaged building. Vehicles came and went, too, but there was an impression that gradually things were growing calmer.

'You were in the building?' Madeleine asked a woman, who was trembling, sobbing and stammering incoherent words, as she stood helplessly in the middle of the mêlée.

'Yes, but . . . you're speaking English! Oh, dear

God!' She collapsed on to Madeleine's shoulder and did not resist when she was led into the now-brightly-lit kitchen.

'Are you hurt?' Madeleine asked.

'I don't know—I'm cold. Look, I'm shivering.' Her teeth chattered from shock and lowered body temperature.

Madeleine turned to André Durant, the man who had helped her to set up the kitchen as an emergency area.

'That's something I forgot,' she said. 'How stupid! We'll need blankets—as many as possible. There must be spare ones in the hotel.'

'I'll go straight away. Any special kind?'

'Pure wool. That's far preferable to synthetic fibre. Sheets, too, perhaps.'

'Right.' He hurried off.

Madeleine returned to her examination of the distressed woman and found that she appeared unhurt, apart from a bad graze on the leg where she had evidently blundered into something in her frantic attempts to get out of the burning space. Madeleine dressed the area with disinfectant and gauze, guessing that a huge bruise would develop beneath it, but thankful that the women's injuries were not worse. She must have been one of the first to escape from the building.

'My husband! He's who I'm worried about,' the woman desperately said as Madeleine was about to leave to attend to three more people who had just been brought in. 'I haven't seen him. I think he got out. He pushed me in front of him, so he was quite near me, but right at the end—there was such a crush, people were screaming. I don't know.'

'Try not to worry.' It was terrible how helpless and trite the words sounded. 'He's likely to come here when more people realise it's been set up as a first-aid centre,' Madeleine told her. 'Or if he's been more seriously injured, he'll be on his way to hospital by ambulance.'

'But if he was trapped inside! Was anyone trapped? Have people died?' The woman was becoming almost hysterical.

'We . . . we don't know,' Madeleine was forced to say. 'Try to drink your tea . . .'

She had to turn away to help others now, but she felt very bad, memories of her own loss eight months ago coming back vividly in this crisis.

'I mustn't think of it,' she said aloud.

The next people she treated were all suffering from cuts, grazes and bruises, one with a badly bleeding forearm which he had apparently gashed against a broken piece of the mirrors which had formed much of the décor.

'It was terrifying!' another woman told Madeleine. 'Those mirrors! There was smoke. It was just before the lights failed, and I couldn't see what was real and what was a reflection. I thought I was going to crash into glass, having thought it was an escape. Like Alice Through the Looking-Glass gone all wrong!'

She began to sob, and Madeleine shivered, then felt a hand on her shoulder. It was Christian.

'I can't stay,' he told her. 'I'm needed. I just came to tell you that a doctor and a nurse from Antibes will arrive at any minute to help here . . . and that you are doing a fabulous job.'

He squeezed her hand quickly between his two very warm ones, and then was gone again as quickly as he had come, leaving Madeleine profoundly disturbed at the contact between them. But she was still far too busy to think of it. It was evident that smoke inhalation was going to be a problem, and several people had now arrived who were obviously suffering after inhaling toxic fumes given off by the synthetic fibres and plastics of the décor in the nightclub.

The French doctor and nurse had arrived now, and were soon at work, using adequate English when necessary. Madeleine made two more trips back to the chaotic scene of the fire in search of people who were too dazed and shocked to find the first-aid station for themselves, and each time brought back two people, but on her third trip she could find no one, and guessed that all the people who needed help had now been reached.

She had time to look around quickly for Dr Galantière, but could not see him, and she wondered vaguely what she would do if he had gone back to Le Breuil without her. The fire was fully under control now, and almost out, but many people still milled around the area, shouting to each other urgently.

Madeleine returned to the first-aid station and worked solidly for some time longer, bandaging and dressing cuts and grazes, soothing and calming traumatised people, and giving instructions. She saw that the first woman she had treated was still there, sitting in a corner and sobbing, only now it was with relief. Her husband had come in and had been treated for only one minor burn. Madeleine sent up a little prayer that everyone would find the people they loved soon.

It was light before the work showed signs of slowing down. Several people had been taken from Madeleine's area to hospital, either in Le Breuil or in Antibes, some had been allowed to return to hotel rooms or lodgings in nearby resorts, and others were still seated in the makeshift emergency area, wrapped in blankets and sipping tea, before they became calm enough to leave.

'Take a break, Madeleine, and have some tea yourself,' Dr Galantière said softly beside her, as she sat with a young man of about twenty, who was still very distressed and seemed to need to talk out his experience in minute detail to calm himself down.

'I'm all right,' Madeleine smiled up at the surgeon, but was aware that, now things were becoming calmer, lassitude was creeping in.

'You had already worked a full shift this morning,' Dr Galantière said. 'You need to rest.'

'What about yourself?' Madeleine retorted.

'I intend to. See, I've brought us each a cup.'

At that moment a middle-aged man and woman walked into the emergency area and came across to where Madeleine and the injured young man were sitting.

'Malcolm!' The woman enfolded him in her arms, and it was obvious that they were mother and son. 'Are you all right?'

'Ask the nurse here,' he managed to reply shakily.

'He is,' Madeleine assured the young man's mother. 'He's had a shock, and there'll be a few bruises.'

'Can I go home now?' asked Malcolm, much calmer now that his parents were here.

'Dr Galantière?' Madeleine turned to him.

'Are you in a hotel room?' the doctor enquired.

'No, holiday flats,' the young man's father put in.

'Then I don't see any problem,' Dr Galantière decided. 'Take him with you now. You'll need rest, of course, Malcolm, but a holiday flat will be more comfortable than here.'

The three left, and Dr Galantière turned to Madeleine again.

'Ready for that tea? It should still be hot.'

'It would be lovely,' Madeleine admitted, gratefully accepting the cup he passed to her.

They sat in silence for a few minutes, then Madeleine spoke.

'What's going on? Are there . . . did anyone die?'

'We're ninety-nine per cent sure that no one did,' Dr Galantière replied. 'It's something of a miracle, actually. The place is in bad shape, but I managed to get a bit of a look and I would say there were forty very lucky people in there tonight. The exits are confusing, and the whole place is cluttered with fixed mirrors and screens. The only thing that saved some of those people is that the lights failed relatively late in the piece, and the disc jockey had the presence of mind to throw open two emergency air vents which let a good proportion of the toxic fumes escape.'

'And is the disc jockey all right?' asked Madeleine.

'He's one of the six who were seriously burned,' Dr Galantière replied gravely. 'We have him and two others in intensive care in Le Breuil. The rest are in Antibes.'

'How many were hospitalised altogether?'

'Nineteen. But most should be out within a week or two.'

'What happens next?' Madeleine asked.

The doctor considered for a moment, looking about him. The doctor and nurse from Antibes had left fifteen minutes earlier with the last two patients who needed hospitalisation. Five people were left in the kitchen now, all sitting or lying down quietly, as well as André Durant, the efficient young employee of the holiday complex.

'These people will be ready to go soon. They just need a day or two of bed rest and peace and quiet. We'll need to tidy up, then we can go back to Le Breuil.'

Half an hour later the first-aid area was quite quiet. Madeleine repacked the first-aid supplies which had not been used, ready for putting in Dr Galantière's car. The surgeon, with apparently no regard for the dignity of his profession, helped André Durant to clear up dirty tea-cups, empty milk cartons, and other articles which had been used or disarranged by the presence of the casualties.

It was all completed in a remarkably short time, and Madeleine was almost sorry. There had been something very peaceful about this aftermath to the long night. The sun had risen now, and fingers of clean morning light were beginning to filter into the landscape. Madeleine could not help glancing frequently at Dr Galantière, her heart touched by a sharp pulse each time. It was disconcerting once or twice to find his eyes caught with hers in passing. On these occasions she looked away quickly, pretending to be very busy with her hands. They did not speak to each other, except when it was necessary to ask a question or make a suggestion, but Madeleine was constantly aware that he was here, and that she loved him, even though she knew he did not feel the same.

'Can I be content with this?' she wondered. 'To snatch at tiny moments in his company, and watch him find someone else one day? I was wrong about him before. He isn't a man who will be content to stay alone for ever, with nothing but his work. He's just waiting for someone very special, and one day he'll find her.'

Madeleine thought tiredly about the possibility of going back to England. She had planned vaguely to stay here for some time, possibly even years, but she had not considered how she would feel about Le Breuil if she fell hopelessly in love here. How could she have? Any dreams she had half-consciously dreamed about such a thing were about romance that culminated in shared love, not this awful knowledge that Christian Galantière did not return the passions he had aroused in her.

Mentally, Madeleine shook herself out of the mood. She was very tired, and that was making things blacker than they need be. It *would* be possible to stay on here. There were other things to capture her interest, even though she could not have love.

'Madeleine! Madeleine?'

She came out of her reverie to find that Christian was standing beside her, a crooked smile of perplexed amusement on his face.

'Were you asleep on your feet?' he asked. 'I've been watching you roll and unroll that bandage five times, and when I called your name, you seemed not to hear.'

'Did I? I must be tired.' She summoned a smile.

'We're ready to leave. There are just these three boxes to put in my car. André wants to lock up the kitchen.'

'Did . . . did anything get broken?' Madeleine asked brightly, trying to enter into the present again.

'Nothing,' said André Durant. 'You've been absolutely marvellous. The company will want to thank you officially for all this.'

'There's no need,' she assured him.

'Nevertheless . . .' he beamed at her appreciatively behind round-framed glasses, 'I'd like to thank you *personally* as well.'

'I'm too tired for it now,' Madeleine laughed.

'Of course.' He became suddenly matter-of-fact again, and picked up one of the boxes of first-aid equipment, while Christian and Madeleine followed with the other two.

'I'm supposed to be working this morning,' Madeleine said when they were driving along through the early morning.

'I know,' Dr Galantière replied. 'I've already taken care of that. Jeanne Thierry will take your place . . . In fact, you won't be working on Hibiscus Ward for some weeks.'

'Oh?'

'Two of the serious burn patients we have are English, so I've decided to transfer you to our burns unit. They'll need a lot of support here until they're ready to travel to England for the later stages of their convalescence. As you know, burns can be among the most traumatic of injuries.'

'Yes, I'll be very happy to be in that unit,' Madeleine nodded.

A short while later they pulled into the hospital driveway and Dr Galantière parked his car.

'Get a good few hours' rest, Sister Carver,' he ordered.

'If I weren't so far junior to you, I would venture to give you the same advice,' she dared to counter.

'Don't worry, I'll manage something.'

'Well . . . *au revoir*.' She opened the door of the car, trying not to betray her reluctance to leave his presence.

'Yes . . .' he hesitated. 'Sister Carver?'

'Yes?'

'You're a very good nurse!'

CHAPTER NINE

TEARS blinded Madeleine as she went up the steps and started down the long series of corridors that led to her room. She was a good nurse—that was all he had to say to her.

Are you surprised? she chided herself. What on earth made you think he would have anything more to say?

And yet foolishly she had. During the night they had just spent working together there had been no hostility or distance between them, and imperceptibly the conviction had been growing inside her that perhaps it was the start of a new warmth that might lead to something after all. But it had been naïve to think so. Of course he had not had time for hostility. He had been working to save lives, and all he had seen in her was a helper who had turned out to be capable and efficient in a crisis. The scenario she had sketched as they tidied the kitchen, about the other woman he would soon find, had been the correct one.

She was a good nurse. After everything that had passed between them, that statement was the summing up of Christian's feelings for her.

'Madeleine Carver, go to bed and get some sleep,' she ordered herself grimly. 'And if you have to think about this stupid subject at all, think about it when you're emotionally fit to do so!'

It was four in the afternoon when she woke after a heavy sleep that had been undisturbed even by dreams. She was unsettled by the dislocation in her timetable. It was not like being on night duty, when she would have known she was to be on the ward later that evening. Dr Galantière had said that she was to begin work in the burns unit, but he had not said when, and he was the last person she felt like asking about the matter.

She slipped down to the bathroom, hoping that a cool shower would revive her enough for her to decide what to do, and met Julie Rondin on the way back.

'You're in your dressing gown too!' Madeleine exclaimed.

'Yes. They roped me in to help with the casualties last night—or this morning, rather.'

'How was it?'

'Well . . . terrible, amazing. I've never worked in such an emergency before. It was gratifying to feel an important part of something so urgent. They say everyone is doing remarkably well, and that it's a miracle there were no deaths.'

'Yes, I'd heard that.'

'Although apparently one of the people taken to Antibes is likely to be on the critical list for quite a while. You were part of it all too, weren't you? You were actually there?'

'Yes, although it's already beginning to seem like a dream.'

'Two of Laurent's friends were slightly injured in the fire,' Julie said, pronouncing her boy-friend's name with a special intonation that gave Madeleine a curious pang of envy. 'When he heard about it this morning, he rang me up straight away and said he thought we ought to get married—this was at seven in the morning, mind you! I'd only just finished working,' Julie laughed.

'Strange circumstances for a proposal,' Madeleine agreed. 'Did you accept?'

'Of course.'

'You're very happy?'

'Now, I am. Then I was too tired. Shall we go to the beach and talk? I feel I need some fresh air, and a good gossip. I'm back on my usual ward at seven tomorrow morning? When are you working again?'

'I don't know,' said Madeleine. 'Dr Galantière told me I would be going into the burns unit to be with the seriously injured patients there—two of them are English. But he didn't say when I was to start. Should I go and ask?'

'I don't think so. He'll send a message, won't he?'

'Yes, I suppose so.'

She and Julie had their gossip on the beach, and after the evening meal, Madeleine walked into Le Breuil village for coffee at the café with a group of younger hospital staff members. They had done this a few times before, and Madeleine found it a pleasant way to spend an evening, as well as a good opportunity to practise her rapidly-improving French in what she still found the most testing circumstances—lively slangy conversation. Back in her own room later, she read a book for quite a while, being too wide awake after her long sleep during the day to go to bed again so soon.

Eventually she did sleep, however, to be wakened by a knock at her door the next morning. It was one of the office staff.

'Dr Galantière wanted me to tell you that he would like to see you in his office as soon as possible,' she told Madeleine.

'Urgently?'

'Oh no, I don't think so. When you've eaten.'

'Actually I think I'm too late for staff breakfast, but it

doesn't matter. Thank you for bringing the message,' said Madeleine.

She assumed the surgeon wanted to tell her about her new working arrangements. Was he planning for her to start this morning? Perhaps she ought to wear her uniform. She decided against it in the end, thinking it was unlikely she would have to start immediately. It would only take a few minutes to return and change if necessary.

Instead, she chose a bright and pretty red and white sundress she had recently bought on a shopping expedition with Julie, hoping that the cheery colours would help to take her out of a mood which was still negative and lethargic.

'Madeleine! Good!'

The doctor's greeting was brisk and businesslike when he opened the door of his office to find her standing there. Madeleine's heart twisted painfully at the sight of him and she felt tightness clutch at her throat. How long would it be before she could learn to control her reaction to him? She was so aware of his body in its casual yet well-fitting clothes—black denim trousers and a short-sleeved tropical-patterned shirt.

'So you want me to start working in the burns unit today?' she asked, to distract herself from her feelings for him.

'No, it's not that, actually,' he said. 'I want you to come into Nice with me. The authorities are anxious to start an inquiry on the fire as soon as possible, and they want us to answer some questions about our involvement and what we observed. Later we may have to testify at a hearing. I'm sorry to have let you in for all this.'

'I don't mind at all,' Madeleine assured him. 'If it will

help to prevent such things from happening in the future.'

'That's how I feel,' the surgeon agreed. 'With tourists pouring into this area in greater numbers than ever in future, facilities have to meet certain standards. Are you free to go straight away?'

'Yes, if that's what you would prefer,' she nodded, thinking at the same time that ninety per cent of her contact with Christian seemed to take place in his car. He was probably thoroughly fed up with ferrying her around. How on earth could she have been so naïve as to expect romance to blossom in such circumstances?

They were soon on their way, spending the drive talking in a casual way about the fire and the work that Madeleine would be doing in the burns unit.

'I'm a "good nurse",' she thought, 'and that's that.'

They spent over two hours at the administrative building, being interviewed and writing preliminary reports about the near-tragedy of Saturday night. Madeleine could not help being aware every moment of Christian's cool capability in this situation. He answered every question clearly, and was obviously on good terms with several of the officials.

'He's quite an important figure in this area,' she realised, thinking back to the time she had been at Tanya and Serge Garcia's and he had arrived, evidently valued as a professional man by his hosts and their guests.

'We would be too late for lunch at the hospital,' said Christian, looking at his watch, as they emerged from the building into a day which was by now quite hot.

'Do you think so?' queried Madeleine, consulting her own slim silver timepiece.

'I've packed a picnic,' Christian replied, 'so I don't want to hear any arguments.'

She flushed faintly as she met his gaze.

'He's thinking of that other picnic we had,' she realised. 'The time we kissed.'

Was he going to try something of the kind again? Didn't he know that that would be just a travesty to her when she wanted so much more? She knew she ought to insist that they return to the hospital, but she did not have the emotional strength. Christian was speaking again.

'I'm going to put the top of the car down, it's such a glorious day. We'll go out along the Corniche road towards Menton. We'll have the breeze in our hair. You'll love it.'

Madeleine distrusted the enthusiasm of his tone, but once they had started moving again she became lost in the pleasure of the drive, until he turned off the road, wound down through a hilly village and found a beach.

'Here?' she said.

'Yes. Do you like it?'

'It's gorgeous!'

Unwillingly, she helped him with the picnic rug she remembered so well, and with the cane picnic hamper he produced from the boot. He was setting up this scene as a repeat of the last time, she was sure of it now. What did he want to try?

Minutes later they were settled on the sand. Madeleine looked out at the water, refusing to meet or respond to the smile she knew he had turned on to her.

'Are we going to eat, then?' she asked stonily.

'Soon. Is there any hurry? Are you starving?' he queried with a beguiling smile.

'Yes.'

'What's the matter, Madeleine?' His voice was low and he had moved very close.

'Please stay away!' she said desperately. 'Let's get this picnic over and get back to the hospital. You must have work to do, surely?'

'It can wait.'

His arms were around her now, insistently pulling her towards him.

'No!' The word broke from her lips as a chocked sound.

'Madeleine, why?' But he had released her.

'Don't you have any understanding of how I must be feeling?' She turned to him, ablaze with anger and hurt. 'Don't you remember that all this has happened before? Near Lyon that day?'

'Of course I remember.'

'Yes. But evidently your memory isn't the same as mine,' she retorted. 'I remember how you kissed me then, made me respond. I thought it was the start of something between us, and then a week later it was as if we had never met. Do you think I'm going to respond to you now, and have to go through your rejection all over again, when you've grown tired of your bit of fun?'

'Madeleine, my darling, my dearest darling!' His arm had snaked around her again and this time she could not find it in herself to pull away. 'Somehow we've been misunderstanding each other for weeks. Haven't you guessed that I love you? You can't go on thinking it's something fleeting. You must tell me if you feel the same way.'

For a moment she was stunned into paralysed silence, unable to believe that he had really spoken the words.

'Say it again,' she whispered, her lips pressed against the shoulder of his shirt.

'I love you. I want you to marry me,' Christian whispered. 'I felt weeks ago that it was you who rejected me, and now you're saying I was the one who turned cold.'

He coaxed Madeleine's head up from his shoulder and found her lips, kissing her so thoroughly that for a long moment she didn't care how they had come to misunderstand each other. Then he pulled away.

'We have to clear this up,' he said, laughing softly and touching a brown finger to the tip of her nose. 'Why did you think I had rejected you?'

'Christian!' Madeleine exclaimed in a disbelief that she could enjoy now. 'We arrived at Le Breuil and you went off into the building, leaving me with Madame Chevet without so much as a goodbye. I was already head over heels in love with you—I admit it now, although I didn't fully realise at the time. I waited for days for you to come and see me—knock on the door of my room, or take me aside on the ward just to give me some sign that it wasn't just a piece of meaningless flirtation for you.'

'So that was it,' he said softly. 'Madeleine, that *is* one of my faults. I can get so caught up in my work that everything else goes blank. I had been away from Le Breuil for three weeks, and when we arrived back there my head was suddenly plunged into problems again. I was going to come and see you that very night, to ask you to come out with me, but there was an emergency operation—you probably never heard about it. Then one of the hospital board members contacted me with some grievance. The days went past and I scarcely noticed, I was so busy. I was thinking of you whenever I could . . . Then I had to go into Marseille. I was absolutely determined, on that Saturday morning when I was driving back, to see you that very afternoon. If you'll believe it, I was going to ask you to come to dinner with me at the Garcias'—it would have made the company of some of those people more bearable!' he laughed wickedly. 'But when I drove into the hospital, the first thing I saw was you with Patrice. You looked happy in his company—I had already experienced the sway he seemed to hold over some of the staff at my hospital,' was his ironic addition.

'I'd given up all hope of you by then,' Madeleine explained.

'Weren't you a little too easily put off?' he suggested, kissing her softly on the forehead to take away any sting from the words.

'I don't think so,' she said slowly. 'You see, I couldn't forget the terrible impression I knew I'd made on you during my interview with you in London. It was easy to believe after that that you'd decided I was a type who could be used for a brief affair, then brushed aside with no ill effects to either person. I was so amazed, in the first place, when you gave me the job, that our weekend seemed like the illusion, and your first reaction to me the real indication of how you felt.'

'You didn't impress me particularly at first,' Christian admitted. 'Why did all that happen, my darling? Why were you late, so heavily made up, and so shallow-seeming?'

'It was all to do with the death of my parents,' Madeleine said softly.

'Dearest, I didn't know about that then.'

'I know. I couldn't tell you. That was why I said that ridiculous thing . . .'

'"Who wouldn't want a job in the south of France?"' Christian quoted.

'Exactly. Coming up to London was one of the first times I'd been able to feel cheerful since it happened. I decided to buy myself some new spring clothes, then I realised my face was so pale, and shadowy as a ghost. I thought you would think I was ill and wouldn't want to take me on, so I had a make-up assistant in a chemists do my face. She took much longer than I thought she would, and painted it much more dramatically—and that's the whole story.'

'You must have felt terrible,' Christian laughed.

'I did. I couldn't understand why you gave me the job. Why did you?'

'Because Thomas Brownrigg had asked me to do so as a personal favour to him. He said you'd had a difficult time, and I assumed, after seeing you, that he meant some kind of romantic scandal at the hospital.'

'The dreadful man! He told me that *I* would be taking the job as a favour to you!' Madeleine fumed, not in the least angry in reality, because if it hadn't been for Thomas Brownrigg's guile, she would never have met Christian.

'I wonder if he had any idea that this would happen,' Christian said softly, kissing her ear as he whispered into it.

'He's no fool,' Madeleine agreed.

There was a contented silence for a moment as they found each other's lips again, this time in a gently exploring kiss that held all the promise of their future together.

'What made you decide that I loved you, Christian?' she asked softly.

'It was very gradual,' he replied. 'I began to hope that you might after we delivered Irène's baby—we seemed to work so well together. Then during the fire I caught your eye so often, I started to feel nearly certain.'

'And yet all you could say to me afterwards was that I was a good nurse!'

'I couldn't find a way to tell you. This morning I thought of this picnic, and even that nearly didn't work!'

'But it did in the end.'

'I'm going to keep telling you . . .'

'That day you apologised about your anger over Monsieur Hébrard's drip—were you trying to tell me something then, too?'

'It was an overture,' Christian admitted. 'I felt terrible about my anger, but it was only that very day that I'd been hauled over the coals by the Chairman of the Board for taking on too heavy a load. Your comment about getting more rest hit a raw nerve . . . But then when I apologised you didn't seem to care at all!'

'Oh, Christian! I cared very much, but I thought you were just saying it to make things bearable between us when we went to Marseille together.'

There was another delicious pause, then Madeleine spoke again.

'There's just one thing I'm worried about now.' She frowned a little. 'You're not going to be *too* absent-minded and involved in your work after we're married, are you?'

'I hope not, my darling,' Christian laughed. 'But I'll tell you this: there are going to be quite a few changes to my life which should help. For a start, I'm going to give up the apartment at the hospital, and we're going to live in Nice. Would you like that? There are some beautiful houses, or a modern apartment. We'll choose something together.'

'That would be perfect!'

'Secondly, I'm going to cut down on my administrative load. It's too much for one person. I'd got into a terrible habit over the last five years of thinking of nothing but work. It was a vicious circle. The less time I had for other things, the less chance they had of capturing my interest. But now I have you—and I think that will prove to be a pretty strong distraction for some time to come.'

Madeleine laughed happily against his chest.

'Oh, Christian! I'm sure there are a dozen more things I want to ask you about what you've been feeling over these past weeks.'

'I know,' he agreed. 'Like this: "What did you mean when you said . . . ?" "What were you thinking that time when we . . . ?" We'll find out those things about each other.'

'Do you know why Patrice de Drabant asked me out?' Madeleine asked after they had kissed each other again. Patrice could be almost a joke between them now.

'Wasn't it because he thought you were utterly beautiful as I do?'

'Not at all. He thought I was utterly rich.'

'How on earth did he come to think that?'

'It was all silly Fabienne with her vivid imagination. She read about some missing American heiress with a similar name, and decided that I was she. She told Patrice and three days later he asked me out. When Fabienne found out her mistake and told him, he was furious, and I didn't see him again.'

'Did you mind?' asked Christian.

'What do you think?' she smiled.

'Still, he's not a pleasant character, and he's done harm to more people besides you. Having him on the scene very nearly ruined things for good between us.'

'I know,' Madeleine said soberly. 'But shall I tell you something funny?'

'What is that, my darling?'

'Patrice was wrong about me not being wealthy.'

'Oh?'

'I'm richer than he could possibly know—' she paused teasingly, 'because I have you.'

On the corner of a woollen rug, a forgotten picnic hamper sat slowly baking in the Mediterranean sun.

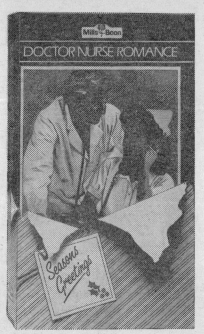

Just what the doctor ordered

The Doctor's Villa
JENNY ASHE

Doctor Knows Best
ANN JENNINGS

Surgeon in the Snow
LYDIA BALMAIN

Suzanne and the Doctor
RHONA TREZISE

Four brand new Doctor/Nurse romances from Mills and Boon, in an attractive Christmas Gift Pack.
Available from 11th October, at £3.99 it's just what the doctor ordered.

The Rose of Romance